SHE SURVIVES

SHE
SURVIVES

Sharon S Darrow

Samati Press

First Edition, 2017
Second Edition, 2020

ISBN 978-1-949125-09-2 (Print Version)
ISBN 978-1-949125-10-8 (Digital versions)
ISBN 978-1-949125-11-5 (Audio version)
Library of Congress Control Number : 2019957584

Edited by Sue J. Clark
Front Cover Design by Leslie Clark

Publisher : Samati Press Sacramento, California

Manufactured in the United States of America

Dedication

This book is dedicated to two amazing women, my mother, June Azevedo, and my maternal grandmother, Laura Schomaker.

My mom shared many incredible stories about her mother, which, together with my memories, were the inspiration for this book.

I love you more than you know, and hope my words honor you both.

I am also dedicating this book to my brother, James Patrick Azevedo.
Pat was one of the kindest, gentlest people I've ever known. He passed away much too soon, but he enriched the lives of everyone who knew him.

Contents

CHAPTER ONE

Hardscrabble Birth

August 1903,
Five miles outside of Ardmore, Oklahoma

Look, Jon, ain't she pretty?"

"She? She? Another damn girl? What's the matter with you, woman.

Five young'uns so far, and only one boy. And him the last a'fore this'n, so he's no use to me on the farm for years." Jon turned away from the bed with a disgusted expression and headed toward the open door. "Pretty? Hellfire, just another useless mouth to feed."

Vera watched her husband shove five-year-old Becca aside as he pushed past his four older children to get through the doorway. He went straight to the wagon, jumped up on the wooden bench and grabbed the reins.

"Miz Dobbs, aint you 'bout ready to head home?" he yelled.

The youngsters, clustered around the open door in the sweltering August midday sun, stared at Vera and Miz Dobbs. They were careful to not look back at their father, hoping he wouldn't focus his attention on them. Ruth, the oldest, made sure Lizbeth and Becca stayed just outside the threshold where Miz Dobbs had told them to remain. She held Ben, just turned three, by the hand to keep him from rushing through the door.

Miz Dobbs patted Vera's arm and shook her head. "I got to go, Miss Vera. Mr. Cavanaugh sounds mighty impatient. You and the baby'll be just fine."

"I know. Thanks for your help. Can't imagine having to birth a baby without you." Vera squeezed the midwife's hand.

Miz Dobbs started to turn away, then looked back and whispered. "Miss Vera, you know your baby was born with a caul on her head. Ain't never seen part of the birth sack stuck to a baby's head like a hat before, but I've heard some folks believe that's a sign that the baby's born with the second sight. Least ways, that's what my gram told me. Do you want to keep the caul?" "I'd love to keep it for Laura when she's grown, but Mr. Cavanaugh wouldn't like it. Would you keep it?" "Yes, ma'am, I'll be proud to keep it for you." Miz Dobbs smiled, packed a collection of bottles, jars, and rags back into her battered leather bag, then hurried out the door.

As soon as she settled herself on the wagon bench, Jon slapped the horse's back hard with the reins. The horse lunged forward into the harness, jerking the wagon onto the rutted road.

Vera waited until the sound of hooves faded in the distance, then pressed her lips against the baby's damp hair. "It's alright, sweet Laura, it's alright. Mama loves you."

Vera stroked the baby's forehead, remembering how she'd looked at birth with the glistening white membrane stuck tight to her tiny head, covering her eyebrows, hair and ears. Poor little one. There should be a ceremony to guide your path and protect you, with all the clan members taking part. "What will it mean for you, my sweet Laura?" Vera whispered in her ear. She knew Laura's life path would be hard, no doubt of that, but she'd also have strength, luck, and special gifts of the spirit. "No tellin' what kinds of gifts they'll be."

Unable to resist their imploring looks, Vera raised her right arm and waved the other children, still waiting in the doorway, to come over to her bed. "Come on now, time to meet your new baby sister."

They rushed forward, jostled for the best positions as they gathered around the bed, stroking the baby's face and arms, holding her tiny hands, and assuring themselves that their ma was alright.

"That's enough for now," Vera said, after each child had a turn with the baby, "I'm awful tired. Ruth, will you fix something to eat for supper? And please close the curtain so the baby and I can sleep."

Ruth nodded, then herded the little ones away from the bed. She closed off the area by pulling together two blankets suspended from a rope stretched from wall to wall just below the muslin-covered ceiling. Something moving on top of the muslin above the bed caught her eye, a clear sign that some type of vermin had fallen through the sod and been caught by the cloth. Wooden pegs, pounded diagonally into the angle between ceiling and plaster-covered sod walls, kept the fabric taut. Ruth could see that Ma would need to replace the muslin soon since it had torn away from some of the pegs and sagged in many places from the weight of the dirt and small creatures it held.

Vera cuddled her daughter's soft, warm body against her breasts. She listened to the faint, whispery sounds of the baby's breathing, then drifted off to sleep, newborn in her arms, both exhausted from the rigors of birth.

Hours later, Vera woke to the sound of her husband stumbling to his side of the bed. She kept her eyes closed and her breathing regular, hoping he'd think she was still asleep. He stank of alcohol and sweat, cursing in the darkness as he pulled off his boots, overalls and shirt, then dropped on the bed and shoved his legs under the covers, still dressed in his dirty long-johns.

Vera heard the children stirring, disturbed by the sounds their father made, before they slipped back into sleep on their straw pallets just a few feet from her bed. Jon's heavy, rhythmic snores let her know when he was asleep, so she could climb out of bed with baby Laura in her arms.

Vera knew the baby needed to nurse but didn't want Laura to wake up enough to cry. Moving in slow motion to avoid making any noise, Vera sat down in an old wooden rocker near the foot of the bed and brought the baby to her breast. Little Laura rooted around for a moment before she latched on and suckled with greed, working her tiny, contented fingers against her mother's skin. As she rocked, soothed by the quiet perfection of the moment, Vera began to sing the Cherokee Morning Song, an ancient melody passed down from one generation to another, just as she remembered hearing it when she was little. She loved the words, but the meaning— I am of the Great Spirit, Ho, It is so, It is so— was even more precious.

> We N'De Ya Ho,
> We N' De Ya Ho
> We N' De Ya, We N' De Ya
> Ho, Ho Ho Ho
> He Ya Ho, He Ya Ho
> Ya Ya Yaaa

She thought only Laura could hear the words, but she was wrong. All of a sudden, her body snapped forward propelled by a hard slap to the back of her head. "I tole you about talkin' Cherokee in my house. If'n I hear it again, I'll knock you clean out'a that chair."

Jon's voice was low, more like a menacing growl than speech. The threat was real as demonstrated by the force of the blow, the promise of more violence clear.

Vera didn't make a sound, nor did she turn to look at her husband. She could sense his presence as he stood behind the chair, looming over her. Squeezing her eyes closed against the pain radiating from the back of her head, she fought against the urge to react. She stayed still, her head bowed forward over her daughter's body, then resumed rocking and nursing after she felt Jon move away from behind her. Within minutes, Vera heard a liquid torrent as he used the thunder-jug from under their bed, then the noisy creaking when he lowered his body back onto the rope mattress. The pungent urine odor stung Vera's nose as she sat, waiting, until his snores once again filled the sod house. Only then did

Vera let the tears run from her eyes while she changed Laura's diaper and rocked her back to sleep.

Vera stayed in the chair a long time, rocking and stroking Laura's warm little body, because she didn't want to climb back into bed next to her husband. How could I have thought he was a good man? If only I'd taken more time to get to know him. There's worse things than being alone.

Jon had first introduced himself at a church picnic. As Vera helped the other women set out bowls of food on long wooden tables, she noticed him watching her from where he stood with two other men. She felt his eyes on her throughout the afternoon, but he didn't speak to her until people started leaving.

"Hello miss, I'm Jon Cavanaugh," he'd said. "You're the schoolteacher, ain't you?"

"Yes, I'm Vera Miller." They talked a long time, seated on wooden benches in the churchyard. She told him about her students, and he told her about purchasing a homestead.

Vera enjoyed talking to Jon and considered him a handsome man. He was tall with dark brown, wavy hair, deep blue eyes, a dark complexion, big, strong looking hands, and a muscular, powerful build. He also had a scar running from just below his right eye to the base of his ear. The scar was pale, a wide, raised welt standing out against his dark skin. Vera tried not to stare, but couldn't help wondering what had happened to him.

Jon was courteous but didn't smile as they talked.

One week after they met, Jon caught Vera at school after her students had all left. He wasted little time before getting to the point of his visit, a marriage proposal. He explained that he needed a wife to help him work his homestead, and she needed a husband. They were both strong, young, and living away from their families. They were also God-fearing, so should share the same ideals about the commandments to marry and raise children. Vera, after a day to think about it, accepted. It seemed like a reasonable decision based on sound ideals, a good match for them both.

Vera remembered her wedding day and wished she could go back and change things. No fancy clothes, flowers, or music, just standing in front of a preacher early in the morning. After saying "I do," she'd watched Jon nod to the parson, then lead the way outside to his wagon, piled high with their belongings. No kiss, no hugs, not even any soft words.

Reaching Jon's homestead had taken all day, and the condition of the place when they arrived was much more primitive than Vera had expected. No house at all, just a crude, three-sided lean-to built into the side of a small hill. She hadn't said a word, though, just followed her new husband's lead, helping him transfer the wagon contents inside and then trying to create some order. When the wagon was empty, Jon put the horse and wagon into the barn which was in much better condition than the lean-to, while Vera started a fire and began to prepare supper. Vera hadn't known what to expect when the sunlight faded, and the darkness drove them inside by the fire. She'd hung a blanket over a rope stretched across the length of the open side of the lean-to, providing them with shelter from the night. When she'd finished, Jon had reached for her without a single word, pulling her toward their bed against the wall. Vera sat down on the thin straw mattress next to him, then was shoved flat on her back and taken like an animal in the field. Vera hadn't fought or protested, understanding it was her duty as a wife to submit to her husband.

Jon wasn't a talkative man, but during long hours trapped together during their first winter, they'd talked about their family histories.

Vera's parents had died in a fire the year before she'd started teaching, only six months after her brother had gotten married and moved away to be with his wife's family. Vera couldn't rebuild the burned buildings or work her father's farm by herself. No clan members lived nearby, and the tribal reservation was miles away. Teaching in a nearby town was her only choice. The previous teacher had married and moved away, so the School Board was happy to accept her. Her education at a Christian off-reservation day school was sufficient for her to teach elementary school students.

Jon's mother had died giving birth to him, her fourth baby. His father had neither the time nor patience to deal with a baby, so he hired a newly freed slave, Millie, to take care of the home and the children, and to serve as a wet nurse. Jon's father had grown up with slaves in the family, so he treated Millie the same way. Jon had one sister, the second oldest child, whom Millie taught about women's work and about a woman's place. Jon's father was a firm believer in punishing youngsters who disobeyed him, using either a razor-strap or riding crop. The scar on Jon's face came from his father's whip, when Jon had tried to turn away once to escape punishment, a lesson he'd never forgotten. When Jon's pa died, the oldest son inherited everything, forcing Jon, his other brother, and their sister to leave and find their own way.

Vera's thoughts were interrupted when Laura started fussing against her shoulder. The motion of the rocker and comforting touch of Vera's hands on her back soothed the baby to sleep. Vera kissed the top of her head. If only they'd talked about family and raisin' young'uns earlier. Never would have married a man with no softness or love inside him. Wasting time looking back though, no way to change things now. Got to get some sleep.

Vera carried the sleeping baby back to

the bed, tucked the warm little body tight against her side, and was soon dreaming, breathing in the sweet smell of her baby's breath.

Vera and baby Laura were together almost all the time for the first few weeks, a cloth sling holding the baby tight to Vera's body. Laura slept to the soothing sounds of her mother's breathing and heartbeat, comforted by the warmth of her mother's voice and body, and the familiar scent of her skin. When Vera needed a few moments without the sling, she would hand the baby to Ruth, always reminding her to hold baby Laura with care.

"I know, Ma, I know how to hold her." Ruth would roll her eyes each time and reply. "I'm nine now, you don't need to remind me every time." The baby took only seconds to settle into Ruth's thin arms, so different from Vera's rounded body. "See, she likes me holdin' her."

"She sure does, Ruth." Vera smiled as she replied, enjoying the sweet picture of her daughters together. "She knows you and loves you already."

Of course, whenever Ruth helped Vera with baby Laura, both Lizbeth and Becca clamored for their turns. "Ruth, you've had her long enough, it's my turn now." Lizbeth always whined. "I'm seven, nearly big as you. Let me have her."

"Me, too. If Lizbeth gets a turn, I do, too." five-year-old Becca would chime in.

Ruth knew it was up to her to handle the two girls' requests. "You can both have a turn, but you gotta sit down first," she'd say, positioning baby Laura into one small lap after another.

Vera never worried about the baby with Ruth in charge. She loved watching and listening to her daughters care for baby Laura, their love for her clear even while they squabbled with each other for their turns. Vera also loved seeing how content the baby was with her older sisters whether Laura was sleeping or watching them with wide open eyes.

"Ruth is quite a little mother," Vera said one day, as she sat rocking and sewing. It was much too hot to work inside, so she'd dragged the rocker and a basket of mending outside and placed them in the shade next to the front of the house. Ruth sat near her, caring for baby Laura. Lizbeth, Becca and Ben played hide and seek, running and giggling, in and out of the barn.

Ma and Pa would've loved them so much. Vera sighed as she watched her children. Near fourteen years and she still missed 'em every single day.

"Ma," Ruth asked, breaking into Vera's thoughts. "Laura is such a pretty baby. What was I like as a baby?"

"You were the happiest of all my babies. Didn't cry, just made little noises right after you were born. Miz Dobbs didn't even have to slap your bottom."

Happy with that answer, Ruth turned her attention back to Laura.

Vera's thoughts drifted back to the day Ruth was one week old. She'd never forget that day, never till the day she died. Vera sat in the same rocking chair where she sat now, bursting with happiness, holding her baby daughter. She'd been singing softly to the sleeping infant, the same song she liked to sing to Laura, when Jon walked over to her.

"What's that song? Didn't sound like no reg'lar words I ever heard," he'd said.

"Just a lullaby my uncle taught me when I was young. Men sing the lullabies in Cherokee culture," Vera answered.

"Cherokee? Your uncle's a Cherokee? You tellin' me you're a damned half-breed?"

Vera stood up and placed the baby into her basket.

"No, I'm not a half-breed, I'm full blood Cherokee." Jon's slap split Vera's lip and knocked her down.

His hands were fisted at his sides as he stood staring at her on the ground, his entire body stiff with rage. "You tricked me into marryin' a dirty Indian? You lyin' whore."

Vera had tried explaining that she'd never hidden anything. It wasn't her fault he'd never seen an Indian teacher before, or an Indian woman who wore her hair up. It wasn't her fault that the Christian name she'd been given by parents educated off the reservation had confused him. He'd never asked, and she'd assumed he knew and didn't care. But her words had no effect. "Iffen anybody in town ever finds out about you bein' a Indian, I'll never live it down. And now my own blood daughter is a stinkin' half-breed? So help me God if this gets out I'll beat you to death myself." Jon's words, spoken in cadence with his fists striking her face and body, left no doubt he meant what he said.

That day was the first time Vera had been beaten. She'd never been hit before, but from then on, she had to endure both her husband's contempt and his thoughtless violence.

Shaking her head, Vera brought her attention back to the present. The past was over. She couldn't change it. Just got to protect the young'uns best as she could.

Vera kept a smile pasted on her face, not wanting her facial expression to invite questions about her thoughts. She watched Ruth handle all three of her younger sisters, moving the baby from lap to lap without ever losing her patience.

Ben, her only son, showed little interest in the baby. It made Vera sad, but she understood. He was three years old and already trying to follow his father's instructions to "be a man." Although his face and body still had the soft contours of babyhood, he almost never let her hold him anymore. And on those rare occasions when he came to her for comfort, he'd pull away if his pa came near them.

Poor Ben. He'd do anything to get attention from his pa. But if he got hurt, all he'd hear was "Stop that cryin'. Men don't cry." If he got caught havin' fun playin' with his sisters, Jon would yell at him, "What's the matter with you, boy, playin' sissy games with girls." And the rare times his pa'd see him huggin' her, Jon'd tell him to "stop bein' a baby."

Sometimes Ben would poke at baby Laura as she rested on one of his sister's laps, but he seldom talked to her or asked to hold her.

And Jon's relationship with the baby? He demanded respect and obedience from his children, not considering affection of any value. Vera took care to keep baby Laura out of his way, knowing it was safer for both of them.

CHAPTER TWO
Harsh Lessons

September, Two years later

The first two years of Laura's life rushed by. The family routines were centered around survival—planting the crops that provided their only cash income, tending the truck garden and fruit trees that fed everyone, and caring for the animals that labored with them to support the homestead and provide meat, milk, and eggs.

Supper was often a tense affair, depending on Pa's mood. His place was at the head of the table, his back toward the curtained off bedroom area, facing Vera, who sat at the other end with her back toward the door. Ruth sat in the middle of a long wooden bench on the side of the table closest to the wood-stove, so she could help Vera with serving and caring for the two youngest. Baby Laura sat on top of an upside-down cooking pot, feet resting on the bench, raised up high enough so she could reach the table between Vera and Ruth. Ben sat on Ruth's other side, between her and Pa. Lizbeth and Becca, big enough to not need help at the table, sat on the bench by the wall, with Becca closest to Vera, Lizbeth in the middle, and an empty space next to Pa.

"Pa," Ben said when his father started eating. "Laura broke three eggs this morning. On purpose."

"Ben," Vera said. "You know she's too young to understand. You're s'posed to help watch her till she knows better." Vera wanted her son to look at her instead of at his father. "And you know better than tattlin'."

"All a'you know better than wastin' food. Three broken eggs means somebody goes hungry. Who was watchin' her?" Jon looked around the table at each stricken face.

"Not me, Pa," Ben said, ignoring his mother's pleading look. "Lizbeth and Becca took her to the chicken house this mornin' cause Ruth was fixin' the dinner pails while Ma threw up."

"Is that true?"

Both girls nodded their heads but knew better than to say anything in their own defense. Ben smirked behind his father's back, after a quick glance at his mother. "Then you should'da been watchin' better." Jon stood up, walked to the middle of the room, and began taking off his belt. "Git over here."

Biting her lip in shame at her inability to stop what she knew would happen, Vera didn't say a word as both girls pushed themselves away from the table, eyes glistening with unshed tears. They trudged to where their father stood, then turned their backs, eyes squeezed shut, hands fisted at their sides in anticipation.

The leather belt struck hard against first Lizbeth's, then Becca's tender thighs, three times for each girl, one stroke for each broken egg. They both cried out in pain, but said nothing to protest the punishment. Tears streaming, painful welts on their legs under long skirts, they sat back down at the table. The rough wooden surface of the bench was agony on swollen, bruised skin protected only by coarse fabric, but neither girl dared cry out or fidget in place.

"And you, little girl, will not break any more eggs," Jon said to Laura, leaning in close to her. He shook his right fist, still partially wrapped by the leather belt, inches from her face as he continued. "You're big enough to learn we don't waste food in this house. Next time this happens, you'll get the strap right along with whoever was s'posed to be watchin' ya."

Vera watched Jon turn away from Laura and walk back to his place at the table, a satisfied expression on his face. After threading the thick leather belt back through the loops in his pants, he sat back down and resumed eating.

Vera didn't dare make a sound or look at her daughters, afraid Jon would consider it interference. And when she glanced at Ben, the pleasure on his face made her feel sick. She kept her face turned away from Jon, eyes darting instead between the untouched food on her plate, and Laura at her side. Vera could sense the fear and tension as she reacted to her Pa's voice.

Laura was too young to comprehend the meaning of Jon's words, but responded to the menace in his tone. White-knuckled hands clenched in her lap, face an expressionless mask, shamed and heart-broken, Vera ignored Laura's little arms reaching out to her for comfort.

From the corner of her eye, Vera could see the shock on Laura's face when she was first ignored by her ma, then by her sister Ruth, whose face and rigid hands mirrored her ma's. Vera remained motionless, but couldn't stop the tears, knowing that for the first time in her young life, Laura had no one to turn to.

I'm so sorry, baby. Vera wished she could say the words out loud. It hurt to sit next to her child, knowing she was shaking and crying, afraid and alone.

God forgive me. What kind of a mother lets a man treat her babies like this? Vera couldn't stop the thoughts racing through her mind. She hadn't always been a coward. She tried, she really did.

Vera closed her eyes and remembered the first time she'd heard Jon say the words, "We don't waste food in this house."

He was talking to Ruth, who'd just dropped a pitcher of milk on the floor.

"She was just trying to help, Jon. It was an accident." Vera remembered saying, as she'd picked up the pitcher and began wiping up the milk with a rag before it could sour into the hard-packed dirt floor.

Jon had taken off his belt, then wrapped it around his hand, the buckle in his palm while the loose end dangled from his fist. Ignoring Vera, he'd grabbed a terrified Ruth by the arm, and swung the belt hard against the squirming, screaming toddler's lower body.

Vera had cried out, and tried to protect Ruth, but Jon shoved her away. She tried to make him stop. She tried as hard as she could, but the more she tried the more he hit Ruth. He only quit swinging when Vera gave up.

She opened her eyes and looked around the table at her silent children, none of whom would meet her gaze. They probably thought that she didn't care, didn't want to protect them. But if she'd said anything, he'd take it out on them. If only they could get away.

CHAPTER THREE

No Joy

May, eight months later

Cold, wet winter storms winter chased fall
away, then gave way to spring. The work was
never-ending for the family, but being able to
be outside in the warm spring breezes was
rejuvenating for everyone. Once the ground
dried up outside, the first business of spring
for Vera and the children was to empty the
sod house for a thorough cleaning.

All the furniture, straw sleeping pallets,
blankets and clothing were carried outside and
aired in the sun to eliminate the heavy, musty
odors from months of being kept inside in the
unventilated air. The pallets, simple bags of
muslin stuffed with straw and sewn shut, were
fluffed as much as possible since they had
packed down from use. Once the house was

empty, they replaced the muslin ceiling with new cloth after they took down the filthy old one and carried it outside with its load of dirt and tiny dried vermin corpses. Nothing was ever wasted, so they added the material to the bedding and clothing piled up outside to be washed. Next, they scrubbed the plaster walls clean of the accumulated soot and body oils. The floor was last. They swept and sprinkled the hard-packed dirt with water to eliminate the surface dust.

The next day Vera tackled the mountain of laundry, the difficult chore made even harder by her huge, swollen belly. In her world, advanced pregnancy was no excuse for not working, so she finished the job before she collapsed with exhaustion that night.

Vera was desperate for sleep, but labor pains started sometime after midnight. She waited as long as she could before asking Jon to fetch Miz Dobbs before he headed out into the fields to work.

"I want Ma," Laura wailed.

Ruth blocked the door to prevent her from getting inside. "No, you have to stay outside." Then she looked at the others just behind Laura. "Lizbeth, you and Becca have to mind Ben and Laura while I help Miz Dobbs. There's plenty of water in the barrel if you're thirsty, and apples in the root cellar if you get hungry 'fore the baby gets here." With those parting words, Ruth closed and barred the door.

She hated shutting the young'uns out, but had no choice. Neither Lizbeth nor Becca could make Ben and Laura stay outside while Ma was birthin' the baby, and Miz Dobbs didn't need them underfoot.

Ruth took a deep breath. She sure wished she could stay outside with them. Leastways, she'd know how to keep them occupied and out of trouble. She didn't know anything about helping to birth a baby.

"Don't dawdle, Ruth," Miz Dobbs called out. "I need your help."

"Yes ma'am," Ruth said as she hurried back to her ma's bedside. "What should I do?"

Ruth couldn't keep her eyes off her Ma's mountainous belly, covered only by a thin cotton nightgown. Ma was on her back in the middle of the bed, hands grasping the edges of the straw tick mattress, knees raised, legs apart. Ma's eyes were squeezed shut, her breath a kind of rapid panting that Ruth had never heard before.

"I'm going to need hot water to keep your Ma clean, and cool water for her face and neck." Miz Dobbs looked back at Ruth, standing behind her. "You're gonna haf'ta help me with the rags too, washin' the dirty ones out. First, though, pull those blankets tight together so your sisters can't see us through the windows."

Ruth pulled the crude room divider closed and immediately started sweating in the sultry air trapped around the bed. The musty scent of the sod house was thickened by the smell of blood and sweat. The only light came through a small window opposite the foot of the bed. Even with the new muslin covering, the ceiling sagged in a few places from the dirt and vermin trapped below the sod roof. Dark spots dotted the hard-packed dirt floor where water had dripped from Miz Dobbs' hands and rags.

Ruth didn't think she could stand bein' in there. She couldn't breathe. "Miz Dobbs," she said, "I'll take these here rags out to wash, then bring you some more hot water."

"Good girl," Miz Dobbs answered. "Best get another bucket of water from the barrel outside too. We're prob'ly goin' to need it."

Ruth stepped through of the blanket divider, then dumped the dirty rags into a basin on the table. She scrubbed the stained rags together in the water, wrung them out, then rinsed them in a second basin. After wringing them again, Ruth draped the rags over the benches to dry out. Protecting her hands with the bunched up fabric of her apron, she lifted a heavy iron pot of simmering water off the stove and refilled a clean bucket. Ruth carried it, swaying from both her hands, to her ma's bedside.

"Here's some more hot water, Miz Dobbs," Ruth said, as she emptied the bucket into a large basin balanced on a wooden crate next to the bed. "I'll go get some more cool water now."

Miz Dobbs nodded as she spoke to Ma, who was moaning and tossing her head from side to side.

It felt good to get out of that room. She sure hoped Ma wouldn't take much longer. Ruth dipped the bucket into the barrel outside the door, filling it with water. None of the little ones were in sight, but she heard faint sounds coming from the barn. She'd better check on 'em later. She wished she could join them outside.

Ruth refilled the pot on the stove, making sure the fire was still burning underneath it, then went back out for more water to refill the cool water basin by Ma's bed. Miz Dobbs didn't seem to notice what Ruth was doing since her attention was focused on Vera. Ruth watched Miz Dobbs place her left hand on Vera's belly, then plunge her right arm deep between Vera's legs under the tented nightgown.

"I, uh, I better go make sure the young'uns are alright." Ruth gulped, as she rushed out through the hanging blankets. She'd seen animals have babies before, but watching Ma give birth was not the same. Ruth found Lizbeth leaning on the barn wall, counting out loud while the others were hiding inside.

Not wanting to interrupt their game, she returned to her tasks inside the house.

Throughout the afternoon, Ruth kept repeating the same steps, keeping the pot of hot water on the stove full, refilling both water basins for Miz Dobbs in the bed area, and tending to dirty rags. She looked for the youngsters each time she drew water from the barrel outside, but left them at their play.

Pa returned to the barn from the fields while Ruth was outside getting water, his presence causing the children to flee and run toward the house.

"No, nothin' yet." Ruth said in response to the unspoken questions as Ben and the girls surrounded her at the water barrel. "Just stay out of Pa's way till he's finished in the barn, then you can go back there and play."

She hoped Pa wouldn't be in too bad a mood, or he'd be after her for sure.

It wasn't long before Pa settled in his chair in the shade next to the side wall of the house. Ruth brought him a glass of water and some cornbread and butter to hold him until supper, then returned to helping Miz Dobbs.

Less than an hour later, she was able to join the youngsters in the barn where they were playing with some kittens.

"The baby's here. A new little sister named Bonnie." "No," Ben shouted. "Pa said this'n was s'posed to be a boy."

"Hush, Ben," Ruth said, grabbing Laura

as the little girl tried to run out the barn door for the house. "No, you can't go see her yet. Ma had a hard time, and we haf'ta let her and the baby rest. Nobody goes in till Pa takes Miz Dobbs home in a little while. And when we're able to go inside, you'll have to promise to be quiet and leave Ma and Bonnie alone."

At long last, Miz Dobbs and Pa came outside, and the children sprinted from the barn.

"I'll get the wagon, Miz Dobbs."

"Thank you, Mr. Cavanaugh." Dismissing Jon as he headed to the barn, Miz Dobbs waited for Ruth to catch up to her. "Do you remember all I told you about how to take care of your ma and the baby? Your pa has to work, so it'll be up to you."

"Yes, ma'am, I remember. I'll take good care a' them."

"I know you will, Ruth." Miz Dobbs started to say more, but the arrival of the wagon ended their conversation. She climbed up on the bench next to Jon, who pulled away without a word or a backward glance. As soon as Pa was out of sight, Ruth led Ben and their sisters to their ma's bedside.

"Come meet your little sister, Bonnie."

Vera's voice was soft and weak.

All five crowded around the bed, jostling one another for the best position, as they stared at the tiny body resting next to their ma's side.

"That's a lot of hair," Ruth said, stroking the damp, silky strands away from the baby's face.

"Look, she likes me," Lizbeth said, pressing her finger against the baby's palm, causing the tiny hand to close.

"Likes me, too," Becca chimed in from her position across the bed from Lizbeth, patting Bonnie's arm.

"Ma," Ben complained, "you know I wanted a brother. Didn't need no more sisters."

"Sorry, son." Ma sighed. "Maybe next time."

Laura wiggled out of Ruth's arms and tried to climb on the bed to join Ma and the baby.

"No you don't," Ruth said, picking Laura up again. "Here, you can see better from up here and not hurt Ma. You don't need to be on the bed."

Within minutes, Ruth heard Pa enter the

house. "Ruth, come on out here and fix some supper." Pa's chair creaked as he settled into it. "The rest of you can help with the cookin' and cleanin' up afterwards."

The children left their ma's bedside to follow Pa's instructions. He never moved from his chair, once again in its place at the table, and didn't say another thing.

Not a word was spoken. Only the sound of eating utensils scraping on the dishes filled the room. When the girls cleared the table, Pa went outside.

Ruth finished all the kitchen chores, pushed the table and benches against the wall, then pulled the pallets from under the bed and unrolled them on the floor. Once the children had all settled down for the night, she blew the lantern out and stretched out on her own pallet. She stayed awake long after the others had fallen asleep, listening to their soft breathing, but she never heard Pa come back inside the house.

CHAPTER FOUR

Worn to the Bone

August 1906, three months later

"I go too," Laura cried, trying to pull away from Vera to follow Ruth, Lizbeth, and Becca through the door.

"No, Laura, you have to stay here with us. You're not old enough for school yet," Vera said, holding tight as Laura fought to free herself and follow her sisters.

"I get to go next year," Ben bragged from his seat on the bench. "But you'll still have to stay home with the baby 'cause you're still a baby, too."

Bonnie, waving her arms from within the sling against Vera's chest, started crying, the last straw for Vera, exhausted by the bickering.

"That's enough from both of you," Vera said to Ben and Laura. "Not another word about school. If you can't find something to do except fight, you can march straight to the garden and start picking bugs off the plants." With that final warning, she walked from the door to the rocker, sat down, and opened her blouse for the fretful baby to nurse.

Both children hated bug duty in the garden, so they stopped picking at each other. Laura settled down in the middle of the floor with her corn husk doll and some of the doll clothes Vera had made her from scraps, while Ben went outside to kick his tired, old leather ball around.

Vera leaned her head against the back of the old rocker and closed her eyes, soothed by the gentle motion. I don't rightly know what's wrong with me, so tired and aching all over. I'd give anythin' for a nap. "Please, Bonnie, just quit fussin' and go to sleep.

I don't know what to do with you." All of her other babies had been happy and easy, but it seemed like Bonnie was always agitated or crying.

As soon as the baby finished nursing,

Vera put her into her cradle and carried it outside. Scrubbing diapers on a washboard wouldn't work well with a baby in the sling.

Vera checked the large pot of water hanging from a tripod over the outside fire-pit that she'd stoked before starting breakfast. Steam was rising from water hot enough to be poured into the metal tub with the washboard securely braced against one side and ready for use. A second, bigger tub, filled with clean water for rinsing, rested next to the one for washing. The rinsing tub did double duty for the family since it also served as their bathtub. Two parallel ropes, pulled taut, ran from the roof of the house to the roof of the chicken coop, ready and waiting to hold the clean laundry that would soon be draped across them.

Vera lifted a basket filled with dirty laundry, grunting with the effort. She hoped all the young'uns behaved so she could get the laundry done. Didn't matter how she felt, neither. She was almost out of clean diapers. Vera dumped the laundry out on the ground to the left of the washtub, then placed the empty basket to the right of the rinsing tub for the clean clothes. Next, she carried the heavy pot of hot water from the fire to the washtub and filled it halfway. Dirty laundry followed the water into the tub, where it soaked while Vera refilled the pot and hung it back over the fire. When both laundry tubs were ready, she knelt in front, holding a cake of lye soap in one hand and lifting the first item out of the water with the other. She rubbed the soap onto the cloth, placed the cake on top of a wooden crate next to the remaining dirty laundry, then started working the soapy material up and down over the ridges of a washboard.

As she scrubbed the laundry, Vera kept an eye on Bonnie's cradle, just to her right. Soon after she started washing, Ben and Laura wandered over and watched the baby's legs and chubby arms flail around. Ben rocked the cradle back and forth so hard he almost flipped Bonnie out.

"Gently, Ben," Vera admonished. "You need to rock gently or the cradle could tip over."

Ben jerked his hands back and walked away, muttering. "Dumb baby. Who cares."

Vera watched Ben walk away, his back rigid and his hands fisted at his sides, and sighed. Oh no. Seemed like everything she said to that boy turned out wrong and hurt his feelin's. Ruth did a better job connecting with him than Vera did. She shook her head, as Laura took Ben's place next to the cradle, staring at baby Bonnie with intense concentration on her face.

"Ma, she's making' faces," Laura said. "Uh, oh, she's cryin' again."

"Watch her for a few minutes." Vera sighed as she stood, stretched the cramped muscles in her back, then headed for the door. "I'm gonna try something." Once inside the house, Vera tore a square from a clean piece of fabric, then spooned a small mound of sugar in the middle. She twisted the material around the sugar and tied it with a string. Next she pressed the tight bundle into a roll and dipped it into a shallow dish of milk.

"Never thought I'd be giving one of my babies a sugar tit," Vera said, shaking her head as she walked outside to the cradle. "Always said only lazy mothers used 'em."

Vera placed the sugar filled material into Bonnie's mouth, pinning the loose fabric to the baby's gown. In seconds, Bonnie was content, suckling on the sweet treat. Minutes later, Bonnie's eyes closed with her lips locked around the milky fabric. She was fast asleep.

Vera resumed her washing but kept an eye on the cradle. She saw Laura head toward the barn, no doubt bored with watching a sleeping baby. Vera could hear faint sounds from the barn as she worked, but paid closer attention when the sounds changed into raised voices. She couldn't understand the words but could tell something was going on between Ben and Laura. With a last quick glance at the sleeping baby, she sighed, rose to her feet and headed for the barn where the sounds of yelling and crying were much louder.

"What's goin' on here?" Vera asked, hands on her hips, looking from one child to the other.

"Nothin', Ma," Ben replied. "Laura's clumsy and fell down. She hurt herself. I didn't do nothin'."

Vera looked at Laura, noting the skinned palms and knees, and the tears running down her face. "How'd you fall, Laura?"

Laura's eyes darted to Ben's face, then back to her ma's. "I tripped, just like Ben said." A fresh torrent of tears streamed down Laura's face as she dropped her gaze and stared down at the ground, biting her lower lip, hands clenched at her sides.

Once again, Vera looked back and forth between Ben and Laura's faces. "You two are not telling me the truth, and I can't abide liars. If you tell the truth, you won't get in trouble, but I'll take a switch to both of you if you don't tell me what really happened."

"He pushed me down, Ma." Laura said, looking at Ben. She crossed her arms, fists still clenched. She stared first at him, then at her ma. "I said I'd tell you, and he said . . ."

Before Laura could finish, Ben jumped in. "I didn't mean to push her. I just kinda ran into her 'cause she stopped in front of me. You don't like us tattlin', so I told her not to tell you."

"Ben called me a baby after he pushed me on purpose, then said he'd tell Pa I broke an egg this morning iffen I told you." Laura moved closer to Vera and away from her brother. "Ben told me he'd show Pa a shell, and maybe say you knew about it, so you'd get in trouble, too. I didn't break no eggs, Ma. I didn't."

Vera crossed her arms and looked down at Ben, who was staring at Laura. His angry face focused on his sister, and his stiff posture were visible proof of Laura's words.

"Ben, if Pa hears about this, you'll both get the strap for fightin' and then lying about it. Is that what you want?"

Ben shook his head no, his face a mixture of defiance and anger, skin flushed and lips tightened into a thin line.

"Alright then." Vera turned her focus to Laura. "You can't always threaten to tell on your brother. You two are goin' to have to learn to deal with each other or stay away from one another."

With those words, Vera pushed both children out of the barn and headed back to her waiting laundry.

Lord, just let me get through this day.

CHAPTER FIVE

Unthinkable

May, nine months later

Days, weeks, and months passed, marked by monotonous, unchanging routines. Pa split his time between the fields, caring for the ani-mals and barn, and the maintenance around the farm, interspersed with rare trips to town. The three young-est children ate, slept, played, and did those minor chores they could handle. Ma's days ran together, every minute filled with her family's needs, the truck garden, laundry, mending, and cooking, her routines varying as dictated by the children's growth and the changing seasons. Only the three oldest girls were looking forward to summer, eager for the school term to end.

"Four more weeks, four more weeks,

then school's over for the summer,"
Ruth, Lizbeth, and Becca chanted, as they
skipped on their way home. The three-mile trip,
marked by wagon ruts through wildflower-
dotted grassland, was an easy trek in the warm
spring days.

"Just wish it was sooner, or that Miz
Gibson didn't give so many tests at the end,"
Ruth said.

"Don't care," Lizbeth said. "I'll be happy
to sleep a little later in the mornin's."

"Ma won't let nobody sleep in, you know
that." Becca laughed. "She'll just send you out
to work the garden instead of school."

"Wait a minute, what's going on?" Ruth
stopped dead, looking at their yard as it came
into view. "That's washin' hanging on the line.
But now? Ma always takes it in after supper,
long before we get home from school.
Somethin's wrong." Ruth started running,
leading her sisters as fast as they could go.

The girls found Ben, Laura, and Bonnie
sitting in the short wild grass between the
house and the barn, playing with Ben's leather
ball. Ruth touched her lips, motioning Lizbeth
and Becca to stay silent, then leaned down and
squeezed Ben's shoulder. "Great job, Ben,

taking care of the little girls. I really need your help with them for a few minutes. Would you watch them for me?"

Ben shrugged, but looked pleased to be asked. "Guess I can."

"Good," Ruth said. "Where's Ma?"

"Sleeping at the table. She's been poorly all day."

Ruth gave his shoulder one last squeeze, then told Laura and Bonnie to stay with their brother. She ran through the open door with Lizbeth and Becca close behind her.

Vera's head lay on the kitchen table, with her face turned to the left. Her arms were resting on the scarred wooden surface, straight out from her shoulders, elbows bent, both hands close to her head. Vera's mouth was open, a line of spittle spilling onto the table, her breathing shallow and labored. The girls could see their ma's face was glistening with sweat, and her hair was wet and stuck to her skin.

"Ma, Ma," Ruth said, shaking Vera's shoulder. "What? What's wrong?" Vera's head jerked upright, eyes glazed and unfocused at first, glancing wildly about the room before fixing on Ruth. "What are you doing here? Oh, no, I must have dropped off. The little ones . . ."

"They're fine, Ma. Ben's watchin' them." Ruth wrapped her arm around Vera's waist and helped her stand up. "Lizbeth, Becca, take the basket outside and get the clothes down. Everything needs to be put away fast before Pa gets home. Hurry, then we need to get Laura and Bonnie cleaned up before he sees 'em."

"So sorry. Just wanted to rest for a minute." Vera swayed on her feet, body trembling, as her hands pressed against the surface of the table. "Didn't think I'd go to sleep like that. Just wanted to rest my eyes a minute. So tired." Vera looked toward the wood stove where a large pot simmered. "Stew's cookin'. All you have to do is put bread, butter, and water on the table."

Ruth kept the girls focused and working hard to get everything done in time. She even found the right words to encourage Ben to do his part by keeping his younger sisters calm and out of the way. She wanted everything to look normal when Pa drove the wagon into the yard.

After putting the horses and wagon away, and washing up, Pa entered the house. What he saw was plates, utensils, glasses, a pitcher of water, and bread in their proper places, and Vera placing a large serving bowl of stew in front of his place at the head of the table. The children were sitting with their hands in their laps, silent.

Ruth watched Pa look around the table, a slight frown on his face. Everything was where it should be, but she saw from his puzzled expression that he sensed something wasn't quite right. His gaze settled on Ma, who was still standing in the center of the room.

"What's the matter with you, woman? You're sweatin' like a pig, and your hands are shakin'."

Just tired," Ma replied, then walked to her chair and sat down.

Minutes later, she jumped up and bolted through the door. No one said a word, even when they heard her heaving over and over in the yard. Ruth stood and headed toward the door to help her ma.

"Sit down," Pa said, his voice soft but threatening. "But Pa, Ma's sick and needs help." Ruth stared at the door, her attention focused on the painful sounds that continued from outside.

"Don't backtalk me. I said sit down. Now." Pa's voice left her no choice but to obey.

Couldn't Pa see Ma needed help? Ruth was desperate to check on Ma, but remained in her chair as ordered. "Ben, what's goin' on?" Pa asked his son. "That pukin' sounds like more than just bein' tired to me."

"She's been tired and sickly all day. Real hot, too,"

Ben answered, then stared at his plate after a quick glance at Ruth.

Vera appeared, swaying in the doorway. "I'm so sorry. Sicker than I thought, I guess." She started to sit down at the table, but jumped back up and ran through the door.

Ruth started to rise and follow her outside, but one look at Pa's glowering face stopped her from moving.

"When you finish your supper, put a pallet down near the door for your ma. I don't need her sweatin', moanin' and pukin' in my bed tonight. Been bad enough with her tossin' and turnin' the last week," Pa said. "Then clear the table, clean up, and get the others to bed since it don't look like your ma can do it." With that said, he stood up and left, heading outdoors.

Ruth finished as fast as she could, clearing things off the table as soon as each child finished eating. Lizbeth and Becca helped get Laura and Bonnie cleaned up, while Ben went outside to join Pa.

Once the chores were finished, Ruth went looking for her ma. She found her sitting on the ground near the water barrel, her back resting against the wall of the house, eyes closed.

"Ma, just sit while we get the young'uns to bed. You just rest. We can do everything. You'll feel better in the morning."

Too weak to protest, Ma nodded, but never opened her eyes.

Back inside, Ruth shoved the table against the wall to make room for the pallets, pulled them from underneath the bed, and unrolled them on the floor. After tucking her brother and sisters in for the night, she helped Ma stretch out on the extra pallet spread next to the door. Only then did Ruth lie down, vowing to be ready if Ma needed her during the night.

Pa shook Ruth awake early the next morning, well before sunrise. "Wake up. I need you to fix me breakfast and a dinner pail while I take care of the stock. Your ma's hotter'n a firecracker, sweated clean through the pallet. No way kin she take care of things today, so you haf'ta stay home to do the chores. Make the others help you."

"Alright, Pa," Ruth said to his retreating back as he went out the door.

Ruth stood, thinking she heard Ma say something. "What, Ma?" Ruth leaned in close to hear better, but couldn't understand a single word as Ma tossed and muttered in her sleep.

Not knowing what else to do, Ruth wiped Ma's face with a cool cloth, hoping it would help.

She'd never seen ma like that before, didn't dare make Pa mad, so she got breakfast goin'.

Ruth moved to the stove and started fixing a stack of johnnycakes, making enough for Pa and the children, as well. While they cooked, she started on Pa's dinner, first spreading butter on a thick slab of cornbread, then cutting three pieces of cold, sliced salt pork. She wrapped each item in waxed paper, then placed it inside a lard can lined with a clean rag. Next she added an apple, then folded the edges of the rag back over the food before pressing the lid into place.

Soon after Pa finished breakfast and left the house, Ruth woke the children, and fed them the warm johnnycakes with honey.

"Ma's not doing good," she told them. "We have to take care of her and the chores today."

"What's wrong with her?" Lizbeth said.

"Don't know," Ruth answered. "If she ain't better in awhile, I'm gonna ride over to Miz Dobbs place and ask for help."

Nothing Ruth did seemed to make any difference. Ma tossed and turned on the pallet, but never woke up. She alternated between burning up, shoving the covers off her sweat-covered body, and then shivering, her teeth rattling with cold from beneath a pile of blankets. Nothing changed all morning, so after dishing out a cold dinner, Ruth decided she had to get help.

"Lizbeth, you and Becca and Ben are gonna have to watch Ma and keep Laura and Bonnie away from her. I'm ridin' the mule to

Miz Dobbs' place. I'll be back as soon as I can."

"Don't take too long. Pa won't like it if you're not here when he gits home," Ben said.

"Don't worry, I'll be back in plenty of time. Help the girls. And Ben, thanks for being the man while Pa's gone."

Ruth returned alone, dreading telling the others that she'd failed to get help. She removed the horse blanket from Daisy's back and put her into the corral by the barn. She stopped for a moment to watch Ben, Laura, and Bonnie as they chased one another in and out of the empty stalls, waving at Ben to stay there with the girls. Then she went straight to Vera's side, joining Lizbeth and Becca.

"Hi Ma, feeling any better?" Ruth was glad to see her awake.

Ma's eyes were open, but she was unable to sit up. "So tired. Hurt all over."

"Just rest, Ma. We're doing alright." Ruth glanced at the other children, then back at Ma. "Are you thirsty?"

There was no response, but Lizbeth brought her a glass of water. Ruth lifted Ma's head while Lizbeth held the water to her parched lips.

After taking just a swallow, Ma's eyes

closed again, and her head sank back down to the pallet. Ruth motioned for Lizbeth and Becca to join her outside.

When the girls were out of earshot of the house, but before Ruth started talking, Ben joined them, followed by Laura and Bonnie. The children surrounded Ruth, the older ones looking at her with pleading expressions on their upturned faces, while Laura and Bonnie grabbed her hands and hung on, seeking comfort from her touch.

"What did Miz Dobbs say? Why didn't she come help Ma?" Becca said.

Ruth sighed, then spent a few minutes composing herself before she was able to answer.

"Miz Dobbs said Ma might have the typhoid, and there's nothing we can do. She works with babies and can't risk coming here."

"But, we have to do something," Lizbeth said through trembling lips, tears flowing down her cheeks.

"All we can do is just try to keep her comfortable, wiping her face and such," Ruth replied. "Miz Dobbs said some folks die and some folks get better, but nobody really knows why."

Ruth's arms circled the terrified youngsters, as they all clung together in a fierce, desperate hug.

Please, please, Ma, Ruth pleaded under her breath.

You have to get better. We need you.

The silent prayer kept repeating in Ruth's mind as she and all the children cried together.

CHAPTER SIX

Unimaginable

Ruth couldn't get Miz Dobbs words out of her head, no matter how hard she tried. From the moment she arrived back home, she spent every possible minute tending to Ma, keeping her clean and warm, feeding her sips of water and soup, telling her over and over how much they needed her. In spite of everything Ruth could think to do, Miz Dobbs' dire prediction came true.

Two days after Ruth begged the midwife for help, she was shaken awake by Pa. "Get up, but don't make a sound." He whispered in her ear. "Your ma passed during the night, and I need your help." Pa's hand remained on Ruth's shoulder longer than usual, but there was no comfort in his touch.

"What?" Ruth jerked awake. "What did you say?"

"Your ma done passed. I know it's hard, but you got to help me ‹fore the others wake up."

Ruth's heart seemed to catch in her throat. She wrapped her arms around herself and began moaning, a low, painful keening sound.

"Hush, keep your voice down," Pa said in an awkward whisper while patting her back. "Your ma's gone, so there's a lot we have to do. You're the oldest, so carin' for the others is your job now. After I tend to the stock, I've got to go to town and make arrangements for a coffin and a grave, but that'll take awhile." Pa paused for a moment, giving Ruth time to begin absorbing his words, then said, "I need you to help me move your ma 'fore the others wake up."

Tears filled Ruth's eyes as she crawled from her pallet to Ma's side and knelt next to her. "Oh, no, Ma, no," she cried, reaching out to touch the still face. Ma's skin was cool and flaccid, with a waxy feel, and her eyes were closed. "No, Ma, please. I need you."

Ruth shook Ma's shoulder, willing her to wake up and smile, and make this nightmare go away.

"Quiet, girl. You don't want the little ones to wake up and start cryin'." Pa glared at her, his voice commanding Ruth back to reality. "Get a clean sheet and spread it on the table. I'll put your ma's body on top, so we can wrap her up. It'll be some time 'fore the grave'll be ready, but we need to do this now."

Pa stopped at the horrified look on Ruth's face, then said. "I know it's hard to tend to your own Ma's body, but we got no choice. Nobody'll come out to help 'cause they're afraid of catchin' the typhoid. You and me got to do it ourselves, but we don't need to wake the others just yet."

Ruth stood, her whole body shaking, and hurried to do what Pa asked. She cleared off the table first, removing a lantern and some mending she'd been working on the night before, then spread a clean sheet over the top, smoothing it with care. Pa placed Ma's body in the center of the covered table and started folding the edges over the body.

"Wait, Pa," Ruth said, placing her hand on his arm. "Please, let me do that part. I, um, I want to tend to her first."

Pa stared at Ruth's face, his expression was clear. He wanted to finish without further delay. He sighed, but then said, "Alright. When I'm done in the barn, I'll head to town. Then I'll be back for you and your ma. Make sure ever'body's all cleaned up and ready. Don't wanna be shamed in front of anybody in town." With those words, he left Ruth alone with her ma's body, surrounded by the sleeping children.

Painful, silent sobs wracked Ruth's body. She had no idea of what to do for Ma, but couldn't bear the thought of never seeing her face again, of just letting Pa wrap her up with no time to say goodbye. Unable to stay on her feet, Ruth sank down on the bench and reached out to take Ma's hands.

Oh Ma, what are we going to do without you? We need you so much. The painful thoughts flowed with the tears that ran down Ruth's face. I'll do my best, Ma, but I don't know enough. It's not fair, I'm only twelve, Ma. I can't do it. Please, please wake up.

A low moan escaped her lips as she felt Ma's cold fingers beginning to stiffen as she held them. She'd seen enough animal deaths to know there was no turning back now. This was real, this was final.

With a deep, shuddering breath, Ruth regained control of herself. She looked at Ma's body, her gaze lingering at each familiar feature. Ma's mouth and cheeks had crusty streaks of saliva on them, and her hair was a dried out looking, tangled mess. A sour smell came from the body, which Ruth knew would get stronger with each hour.

Guess there's no changing things. But Ma wouldn't want anyone to see her like this. With a final sigh, Ruth moved away from the table to fetch a bowl of warm water and some clean rags.

Ruth washed and dried Ma's face and closed her lips, holding her jaw a moment to set it in place. She'd been helping Ma cool off with wet cloths for the last few days, so this task felt familiar. But when she began cleaning Ma's hands and arms, it didn't feel right, like she was invading Ma's privacy. It seemed wrong touching her like this. Ruth pushed the nightgown sleeves past Ma's elbows and rubbed a warm wet rag down her arms and hands. Ma had such pretty hands. Ruth wished she had her long slender fingers instead of her stubby ones. She wiped each hand clean with care, but couldn't remove the thin dark line under each fingernail. Ruth had never noticed all the scars on her ma's hands before, nearly as many as Pa had.

When Ruth finished with Ma's hands and arms, she folded Ma's arms so her hands rested on her chest, one crossed over the other. Ruth wished she could change Ma's nightgown, since the one she had on was dirty, but nobody was around to help her and she couldn't do it by herself. She hoped ma would understand.

Next Ruth turned her attention to Ma's legs and feet. She couldn't bring herself to raise the nightgown past Ma's knees, so she just washed her lower legs and feet. Thick calluses covered the bottom of Ma's feet, just like the rest of the family's, since she seldom wore shoes at home.

Ma hated having to shove her feet into shoes when she went to town even if they were kind'a pretty. First thing ma would do when she got inside the door was sit down and take off her shoes. The memory made Ruth smile.

Ruth's thoughts were interrupted by the sound of Becca's voice from the pallets behind her.

"What's Ma doin' on the table?" Becca was sitting up and rubbing her eyes.

Before Ruth could answer, Lizbeth and Ben sat up, too, awakened by Becca's voice. All three joined Ruth next to the table, gazing at their ma's body.

"Ma's dead." Ben said, his voice quivering. "Can't you see she's dead?"

"No, Ben. Don't you dare say that," Lizbeth cried, shoving him away with her clenched fists. "You take that back. Ma's not dead, she's just sleepin'."

"Is too dead," Ben said, pushing her back.

Becca, ignoring the others, reached out and started shaking Ma's arm. "Wake up, Ma, wake up. Please wake up, please."

Ruth separated Lizbeth and Ben, then pulled Becca's hand away from Ma. "Stop it. All three of you, just be quiet." Taking a deep breath, Ruth continued. "Please let the babies sleep a little longer. They don't need to see Ma like this."

Ben and the girls started to cry as the awful truth began to sink in. "Please, be quiet." Ruth reached out to pat each of them. "We have to take care of Ma now. Nobody'll help us, 'cause Miz Dobbs probably told everybody Ma had the typhoid. You can help me brush her hair and wrap her in the sheet. Pa's gone to get a coffin and get things ready for the burial."

Just as Ruth finished, Laura joined the others at the table. Confused to see Ma stretched out on top of the sheet, she climbed on the bench and started pulling herself up to join Ma.

"No, Laura." Ruth said, grabbing the little girl and putting her back on the floor. "You can't get up there."

"But I want Ma." Laura tried to get around Ruth and climb back up.

Before Ruth could settle Laura down, Bonnie's wails filled the room.

"Stop it, all of you! I want Ma too, and I know it ain't fair she's gone," Ruth said, her loud, insistent tone getting everyone's attention. "Ma's dead, and there's nothing we can do about it, no matter how much it hurts. We've got to help each other, now, we're all we've got. You know Ma wouldn't want us fallin' apart like this and fighting with each other. I need all of you to help so when Pa gets back from town everybody's cleaned up, dressed, and ready to go to town to bury Ma."

It wasn't fair. Ruth just wanted to lie down and cry. They were all lookin' at her for answers, but if everyone wasn't ready when Pa got back, he'd be yellin' at her. Painful, rebellious thoughts raged in Ruth's head, but didn't stop her from doing what needed to be done.

Ruth handed the hairbrush to Lizbeth and said, "Here, you and Becca take turns and brush out Ma's hair. You know she always kept it smooth and neat. It's an important job for you two."

"Ben, would you watch Laura and Bonnie while I make some breakfast mush for all of us? You're the big brother, the man of the house while Pa's gone. I need your help."

Ruth's words got the children focused on the chores she assigned them, moving their attention away from the helpless feelings of grief that threatened to overwhelm them all.

When breakfast was over, each child said goodbye to Ma in their own way. Just as Ruth folded the sheet up over Ma's feet, Becca rushed over, a yellow ribbon in her hand. "Here," she said, shoving the ribbon into Ruth's hands. "Ma gave this to me, but I want her to have it now."

Ruth took the ribbon and placed it in Ma's hand lacing it through her fingers with care. "That's sweet, Becca, I know she'll like that."

Each of the others brought Ruth their most prized possessions, Lizbeth's lace-edged hanky, Ben's blue marble, Laura's white bird feather, and Bonnie's pink quartz stone, all of which joined the yellow ribbon in Ma's hands. Ruth added her own treasure, a tiny square mirror, to the collection.

"There, now Ma has something special with her forever from each of us," Ruth said. "Come help me wrap the sheet around her."

After Ma's body was wrapped as neatly as possible, the children tucked the sheet in place with gentle pats. They all stood around the table, staring at the cotton shroud that surrounded Ma's body.

"Come on," Ruth said. "We need to get dressed so we're ready to go to church when Pa gets back."

"But it's not Sunday. Why do we have to go to church?" Lizbeth said. "I hate church. It'll be awful without Ma there."

"Hush," Ruth said, "Ma wouldn't like to

hear you say that. 'Sides, I don't think funerals are the same as Sunday services."

Ruth and the others had accompanied their parents to church each Sunday because it was expected of the family, but no one enjoyed it. Pa's place was at the end of the pew on the aisle, so nobody could get out without his permission. Ben sat next to Pa, then came Ruth and the other girls. Ma was trapped at the end by the wall where she could watch the youngsters but couldn't protect anyone from Pa. They all had to sit still through the services, no talking, no nothing. And when the sermon was over, Ma and the children would go straight out to the wagon and wait. Sometimes Pa took a long time, but it didn't matter. They'd all have to be in that wagon, waiting, when he was ready, or he'd get out the belt when they got home.

When Pa returned from town, Ruth met him just inside the door. "We're ready, Pa." They both looked at the table. Vera's body was wrapped in the sheet, and the little ones, all dressed in their church clothes, huddled around the table. Faces streaked with silent tears, they held on to each other for comfort.

"We need to tie the sheet in place," Pa said, as he slid a piece of rope under the body and secured it around the still figure. When the job was done, he picked up his wife's body, now rigid in death, and carried it outside, followed by his silent children. A plain pine coffin waited in the wagon bed, the lid propped on edge against one side. The back of the wagon had been removed and leaned against the back edge of the bed, forming a ramp. Pa carried Ma's body up into the wagon, placed her inside the coffin, and then nailed the lid shut.

Ruth jumped at the sound of each hammer blow as she stood surrounded by Ben and her sisters. The girls all started crying, unable to hold back the choking sounds as they watched Pa fasten the coffin lid in place. Ben didn't cry, but Ruth could see his hands, clenched so hard his knuckles were white, were shaking.

No, no, no more, Ruth said to herself each time the hammer pounded against the wooden lid. She couldn't breathe, just knowin' Ma was in there. It wasn't right to nail her in there, all alone. It wasn't fair.

Pa secured the back of the wagon and walked around to the front. "Come on now, we gotta get to town to finish this." He jumped onto the wagon bench and grabbed the reins. His eyes were dry, but his voice was softer than usual. "Ben, you sit up here with me. Ruth, you and the girls get in back."

Ruth helped the others climb up first, then sat on a bench against the side of the wagon. She held Bonnie on her lap, with Lizbeth holding Laura on her right side toward the front of the wagon, and Becca on her other side, all as close to one another as they could get. The girls didn't talk at all during the long ride. Their backs leaned against the side of the wagon, their sides pressed against each other, bodies swaying and bouncing as the wagon moved over the rutted road. All the girls' faces were swollen with tears, as they stared at the wooden box that rode inches from their legs. It just don't seem possible to Ruth that Ma was in that box, nailed in forever, soon to be deep in the ground. Like God made some awful mistake

Pa drove the horse past the small,

clapboard church, through a narrow path between the headstones, all the way to the back of the cemetery grounds. The grave was on a flat spot in the very last row, in a straight line from the back door of the church. Two gravediggers waited behind the building, leaning on their shovels. They were too far away to hear the preacher's words, but watched for when it was time to complete the burial. Only the minister and a tiny group of townspeople stood near the open grave, waiting for the wagon's arrival.

Pa brought the wagon to a stop near a stunted tree growing in a small, fenced-in family plot. He tied the horse where she could remain in the shade during the service. As soon as the wagon stopped moving, Ben climbed down to follow Pa, while Ruth helped her sisters to the ground.

None of the townspeople wanted to get too close to Jon and the children, afraid that Vera might have had typhoid. The yawning grave with its mound of loose, dark earth separated them from the family, until three of the men looked at one another, then broke away from the group. Without a word, they walked to the wagon and helped Jon lift the coffin out. Together, two on each side, the four men carried it to the graveside. The children, Ruth in the middle with the others clustered around her, followed the men, eyes riveted on the pine box that held their ma's body.

"It's alright. Try not to cry. This won't take too long, then we'll go home," Ruth whispered as they walked behind the procession. She tried to hold back the tears, knowing the others were depending on her strength.

When the men reached the grave, they threaded ropes under the coffin and lowered it into the gaping hole. Pa stayed on the same side of the grave as the youngsters. The men who'd helped him moved back to the side with the other townspeople.

As Ruth watched the coffin being lowered into the open grave, she held on to her composure by remembering Ma's words. She always told us we'd go to heaven when we died. Don't think of her in that awful hole. She's with God now, up in heaven with the angels. It helped some, but Ruth still couldn't control the tears that coursed down her face or the trembling that shook her body. She heard the children crying around her, but was overwhelmed with pain and helpless to comfort them.

Ruth tried to listen to the minister's words, but all she heard was a meaningless buzzing sound. He always sounded the same, every Sunday, talking on and on and on about sinners and hellfire. He'd better not say nothing bad about Ma.

Poor Bonnie, just a year old, had no Ma now. She wouldn't remember Ma at all. Ruth held the baby in her arms, swaying back and forth, as she rocked the little body. She rubbed Bonnie's back, trying to keep her quiet. Laura and Becca pressed against Ruth's sides, moving with her as she swayed. Lizbeth held Laura's hand, linking the sisters together. Only Ben was missing from the huddle as he stood near Pa, hands shoved in his pockets, looking lonely and stoic. Poor Ben was trying so hard to be strong. Ruth glanced at her brother. He's hurtin' same as us, but he looks so alone.

Ruth's attention, which had drifted during the minister's words, snapped back when he stopped speaking. Sermon and eulogy over, he turned to Jon and nodded. Ruth watched Pa take a handful of damp earth from the pile next to the grave, then drop it on top of the coffin. The hollow sound of the dirt hitting the wooden box horrified Ruth, making her feel sick inside.

"Ruth, your turn now," Pa whispered to her. "Don't think about it, just do what I did, then help the others do it, too."

Ruth's whole body shook as she obeyed. "I love you, Ma," she murmured, "and I promise to do my best to take care of everybody for you."

Ruth helped her sisters and brother take their turns. Each of the children followed her lead, tears streaming, unable to control their sobbing. After each child dropped a fistful of moist dirt into the grave, Ruth led them back to the wagon, cringing as the shovels scraped the ground behind them.

The only sounds heard on the ride home were the steady beats of the horse's hooves, the creaking of the leather harness, and the swish of the wagon wheels moving over short grass. It was as if they were in a bubble where nothing penetrated—not a single birdcall, insect buzz, or even the whisper of a breeze.

Pa pulled the horse to a stop in their yard. He remained seated while Ruth helped her sisters down from the wagon bench. Ben, his face in a frozen mask of misery, climbed down from his seat next to Pa without a word.

"Ben, help your sisters pull your ma's pallet outside and burn it," Pa said as he drove the wagon back to the barn. "Don't want a pallet somebody died on in the house."

Ruth wanted nothing more than to curl up in a corner and cry, but remembered her graveside promise to Ma. Ignoring her emotional exhaustion, she comforted the youngsters as best she could and made sure they changed out of their church clothes, then folded and put them away in the trunk against the wall facing the foot of Pa's bed. With Ma gone, Ruth wondered if they'd ever go to church again.

Ruth sent the two oldest girls to the chicken coop to feed the flock and check for eggs, hoping to keep them busy, while she helped Ben drag Ma's soiled pallet out into the yard. Laura and Bonnie sat on the grass and watched Ruth's every move as she filled a bucket of water and placed it next to the pallet. Ruth nodded to Ben, then watched him strike a match and throw it on the muslin-wrapped straw. When she was confident that Ben had the fire under control, she took Laura and

Bonnie back inside.

"Laura, would you help me with Bonnie?" Ruth said. "You can play with her and keep her out of the way while I fix supper."

Ruth felt hollow throughout the rest of the day and far into the night. The tears never stopped running down her face, and she couldn't stop sniffing. Her throat burned from holding in the pain that she couldn't express or allow to escape. Ruth wanted to scream, needed to scream, but was afraid that if she started, she'd never stop.

Loud crying, and silent tears alternated with periods of numb silence in the house. The children, who didn't know what to do or how to act, all looked to Ruth for comfort.

How could she make them feel better when she felt so broken inside? She wished it had all been a dream and she could wake up. And if it wasn't a dream, she wished she could go to sleep and not wake up at all. Long after everyone else, Ruth fell into an exhausted sleep, dreaming of Ma.

CHAPTER SEVEN

New World

"W ake up," Pa said, shaking Ruth's shoulder the next morning. "You got to fix breakfast and my dinner, then get started on chores. If you need help, keep ever'body home. School's nearly over anyways, so it don't really matter."

Ruth's eyes burned. She couldn't breathe through her tear-stuffed nose as she dragged herself up from the pallet. She stumbled outside to wash her face, hoping the cold water would help. As she dried her face on the rough towel draped over a hook on the wall, Ruth kept glancing toward town, thinking about Ma, all alone in the churchyard.

No time to stand there cryin' again. Wouldn't be long before Pa'd be ready to eat and head out. She had to get started. Don't know how Ma did it. She was always up workin', sewing or something, when I went to bed, and up cookin' when I woke up.

Once back inside, Ruth looked at the children still sleeping, just visible in the faint predawn light spilling through the windows and open door. She wished she could join them.

Every morning, thereafter, started the same way, with Ruth getting up hours earlier than the others to start breakfast and fix dinner for Pa. She took care of her sisters and brother, did the cooking, laundry, cleaning, and gardening like her ma used to do. Ruth did her best to care for the children while keeping the household together. Both Lizbeth and Becca helped with inside and garden chores while Ben tried to help more with the animals. Laura was too young to contribute much, so she spent most of her time playing with Bonnie.

Summer flew by as everyone settled into new routines centered around Ruth rather than Ma. As fall drew near, Ruth's thoughts turned to the approaching school term. She loved school, especially the way the room looked on the first day each year, polished floor with no scuffs, clean windows without handprints, blackboards with no chalk streaks, and a contagious excitement. She loved their teacher, Miz Gibson, who somehow created order out of a room full of rambunctious pupils, who ranged from the cute little five and six-year-olds up to teenagers taller than their teacher. Ruth loved the sound of voices as students recited lessons out loud. She had always felt free in school, simply a child among other children who learned for the sheer joy of it. It hurt to know she wouldn't be going back.

"Wish I had some new shoes for school tomorrow." Lizbeth sighed as she picked at her food.

"Your shoes are fine," Ruth responded with a quick glance at Pa. "Buyin' new shoes costs money."

"I know," Lizbeth said. "Just be nice for the first day, that's all."

"I wanna go to school," Laura chimed in.

"Babies don't go to school," Ben said, "and you're still a baby."

"Quiet, all a'you." Pa slapped his hand on

the table. "Don't need all this fool talk at the table, and you all know better. Ben, you're helpin' me with some fencin' repairs tomorrow. You can go to school later in the week when the job's done."

"But, Pa," Ruth said, "Ben's s'posed to start school tomorrow. First day of school is pretty important."

"Did you just backtalk me?" Pa's voice sounded surprised and menacing at the same time. He stood, his big hands braced on the table while the muscles in his powerful forearms bunched under his skin. "

"No, Pa." Ruth's voice shook with equal parts of fear and determination. "But it's the first day, and Ma always told us about how important schoolin' is."

Pa's brutal slap against Ruth's face cut off any more words.

"Ow, Pa, please, no," Ruth cried as her head whipped to the side. Warm blood gushed from her nose, merging with a thin stream that poured from her split lip.

Pa's hand slammed against Ruth's face again, back-handing her this time. Both ears ringing, Ruth fought to stay upright, overwhelmed by pain, weakness, and disbelief.

"Your ma is dead, and any hifalutin' ideas she put in your head are dead, too."

It hurt Ruth to see the children's stunned faces as Pa looked around the table at them. "This is my house, and what I say goes. Any a'you backtalk or sass me will get the same thing. Understand?"

Ruth's left eye swelled almost shut, but she could still see the frightened eyes focused on her bloody face, as each child sat in silence.

"Go git cleaned up," Pa ordered Ruth, as he returned his attention to the food in front of him.

Staggering away from the table, Ruth did as she was told. The cold water from the bucket outside soothed her swollen face. It didn't take long for the bleeding to stop, but her heart continued to race long after. Pa's threat rang in Ruth's ears, and it sickened her to think of one of her sisters or her brother being hit in the face. She remembered watching Pa hit Ma many times, but hadn't understood why Ma never even tried to defend herself.

Ruth looked at her face, dark red marks stark against her skin, in the tiny mirror that hung above the wash bucket. I'm so sorry, Ma. I always thought you were too weak to stand up to him. Sometimes it made me mad to see you act like a coward, just letting him hit you and doin' nothing. You let him hurt you to keep him off us, didn't you? Ruth didn't know if she had the same kind of courage, but vowed to do whatever it took to protect her sisters and brother like Ma had done.

With that decision, Ruth went back inside to finish the evening chores and get Ben and the girls ready for bed. She ignored their looks and comments as if nothing was wrong.

The next morning, long before the other children were awake, Ruth was preparing breakfast and packing the food for Pa's and Ben's dinners in metal lard cans. As she pressed the metal lids in place, she realized she didn't know what they'd do without lard cans. She'd never understood why Ma was so careful with them once the lard was gone. Nothing worked as good for dinners, or for fetchin' stuff from the garden. And now she knew why Ma'd get so mad if they dented one or lost a lid.

Pa and Ben got up next to prepare for a long day working in the fields while the rest of the children continued to sleep. Ruth fed them breakfast and handed them their dinners, but kept her head down. She didn't say a word, ignoring the pain in her bruised and swollen face.

Ruth watched Pa and Ben walk out the door into the predawn darkness. Ben turned back toward her for a brief moment as if he were going to say something, but then turned away, looking both lost and resolute at the same time.

Ruth couldn't help but notice how much Ben was beginning to resemble Pa. They both had the same dark brown, curly hair, and the same startling blue eyes. Pa was a big man, tall, muscular, and powerful looking, while Ben was thin and wiry, but Ruth could see a shadow of the man he would one day become.

CHAPTER EIGHT

Enchanted

September 1908, One Year later

"What happened at school today?" Laura always greeted Lizbeth and Becca the same way when they got home. She loved hearing a story or two from her sisters, now eleven and nine, each day.

Laura had learned not to ask Ben, who at seven was much less enthusiastic. Pa considered working on the farm much more important than classwork, so Ben's frequent absences meant that he was always behind the other students, making him self-conscious and defensive.

On the last day of the school term,

Lizbeth, Becca, and Ben ran into the yard laughing with the thrill of freedom. Laura jumped up and down right along with them. Next year she got to go too. She just had to get through summer and then it'd be her turn to go to school.

Summers meant hard work for everyone. Laura seldom saw Pa at all. He left each morning before she got up, spent the day laboring in the fields of corn, cotton, and wheat that the family depended on for food and cash, then came home for supper. The children did their best to stay out of his way, since he was always dirty, exhausted, and short-tempered.

Ruth was responsible for the truck garden and fruit trees, which were the family's primary source of food. The girls helped in the garden with her. Ben worked with Pa, but also did chores with his sisters. Everyone in the family helped care for the horses, the mule, five cows, six pigs, a flock of chickens, the three dogs and the barn cats.

When the first day of school dawned, six-year-old Laura bounced off her pallet seconds after opening her eyes, too excited to stay in bed any longer.

"Yeah! School today," she shouted. "Help me get ready, Ruth."

"Calm down," Ruth said. "You need to eat and wash up first before gettin' dressed."

Laura was ready faster than anyone—Lizbeth, Becca, and reluctant Ben. With her hair in neat braids, face scrubbed, a fresh washed and ironed dress, long stockings, and well-cleaned and polished hand-me-down shoes, Laura stood before Ruth for a final inspection.

"I'm ready. Can't we go now?" she squirmed in front of her sister.

"Remember to mind your manners today, and do what Miz Gibson says," Ruth told Laura. "If you're not sure about something, just check with Lizbeth or Becca, but don't talk or whisper during class."

"I know, I know, you told me already, I just wanna go." Laura stared at the door.

Final inspection over and last words of advice received, Laura and the others grabbed their lard cans. Laura's fingers curled around the handle as she swung it back and forth in delight.

"What's for dinner?" she smiled at Ruth. "Cornbread with honey, a couple of ham slices, two boiled eggs, and a apple." Ruth smiled back. "There's water in the bucket outside of school to wash it down. Don't forget to wipe your hands and face on the rag when you're done. And be careful with that can. If you dent it, the lid won't fit right."

Nodding her head at Ruth's last words, Laura led the others out the door. After a few hundred feet, she glanced back and saw Lizbeth and Becca talking and laughing as they sauntered along, while Ben lagged behind with a glum look on his face. Impatient with the pace of the others, Laura skipped ahead and then back, again and again, for the first half mile. She couldn't keep up that rapid pace for long though and ended up slowing down to walk with her sisters. Although her speed slowed, her excitement never diminished.

"Look, there it is," Laura said as the school came into view. "Hurry, we don't wanna be late."

"We're not gonna be late," Lizbeth responded, as the girls walked faster now that the schoolhouse was in sight. "Everybody's still playin' in the yard. When Miz Gibson rings the bell, we have five more minutes to get inside before she closes the door."

With each step closer, Laura felt her eyes open wider and wider as she drank it all in. The building's weathered, unpainted boards were silvery gray. Two steps led up to a wide, covered porch that stretched the width of the building front, the entire length edged by a picket fence railing with a top board wide enough to walk on. The closed double doors stood flanked on each side by large windows open to the warm air and covered by white curtains billowing in the balmy breeze.

Just as the girls reached the schoolyard, Miz Gibson stepped out onto the porch and rang a large, wooden-handled brass bell, swinging it up and down so the clapper struck the metal on each stroke.

"Get in line with us girls, Laura," Becca said, grabbing hold of her sister's hand. "We'll be goin' inside soon as everybody quiets down."

Laura, bouncing from one foot to the other, waited for the whispers and giggling to settle down in the lines. The boys were on the left and the girls on the right. Laura noticed that it took the boys much longer to stop playing and fidgeting than the girls, but the girls did more whispering. When all the children were quiet and still, Miz Gibson turned and led her pupils into the schoolroom.

Laura was enthralled with everything from the minute she walked through the door, from the blackboards, with shallow shelves for chalk and cleaning rags, to tall bookcases filled with books, to the wood stove and metal bin for logs, to the teacher's desk with her high-backed chair behind it, to shelves filled with supplies, and to an upright piano.

She had a hard time paying attention when Miz Gibson took attendance. The teacher called the new students names first, in alphabetical order. Laura was the second name on the roll. She raised her hand as high as she could. No longer needing to listen, her attention turned back to the riches of the room. Her fingers ached to touch the books that filled the bookshelves. There were only two books at home, a worn and tattered Bible and the Farmer's Almanac, but she wasn't allowed to touch either of them.

Laura didn't understand much from the lessons that day, but she did join the other students and recited out loud with great enthusiasm. Being in the midst of the noisy class was thrilling, but most of all, she loved watching Miz Gibson and listening to her read out loud.

Miz Gibson's voice was like music to Laura, climbing high then dropping down low, sometimes loud and sharp, other times soft and slow. Listening to her kept Laura's attention from wandering. Miz Gibson looked old, with her gray hair in a tight bun, her wrinkled face, and a round body encased in a long navy-blue dress. She was always moving, especially her eyes, which didn't seem to miss anything in the class. To Laura's amazement, she even knew what happened behind her, catching two of the boys playing at the back of the room while she wrote on the blackboard.

The day passed much too fast for Laura, who was not ready to go home when they were dismissed. Her reluctance soon turned into eagerness to tell Ruth about the wonders of the day.

"This was the best day ever," Laura said, when the children started walking home.

"No big deal. Just school." Ben's disgusted voice made his opinion clear. "You're actin' like a dumb baby again."

Ben's comment didn't dampen Laura's enthusiasm, as she skipped along. "I can't wait for tomorrow. Miz Gibson is so nice."

"She is," Becca said, "but just wait until you have to do your spelling and sums on the board. It's no fun when you make a mistake and the other kids laugh."

"Or when she suddenly asks a question from the reading, and you don't know the answer," Lizbeth chimed in.

"Don't care, I love school."

Laura not only loved school, she also loved sharing what she'd learned with Ruth every evening. In fact, sharing with Ruth became one of Laura's favorite parts of the day. She could be too easily distracted to be a great student, but Laura was always excited to participate.

One morning, Miz Gibson sat down at the piano to teach her youngest students the alphabet. "A B C D E F G, H I J K, LMNOP, Q R S, T U V, W X, Y, and Z."

She sang and played the simple tune as the children stood around her.

Laura couldn't take her eyes off the piano keys as Miz Gibson's fingers moved from note to note. She'd seen the piano in church before, but she'd never watched anyone play it. Her attention was riveted to Miz Gibson's hands, her own fingers moving in concert with the teacher's.

"Ruth, Miz Gibson didn't even look at the piano when she played." Laura repeated the story to her patient sister multiple times when she got home from school that afternoon, with awe in her voice. "Her fingers just knew where to go all by themselves. She looked at us while she sang, but her fingers never made a mistake."

"I know. Pretty amazin'," Ruth said, shelling peas into a bucket as they talked. "But if we keep talkin' about Miz Gibson's music, Pa won't be happy. No school tomorrow, so we can talk all you want while we work in the garden."

The next day after she finished the inside chores, Ruth marched out to the barn with Laura and Bonnie, carrying Bonnie and her doll.

About time. Laura didn't think they'd ever finish feedin' the chickens, collectin' the eggs, milkin', and cleanin' up after breakfast. Ruth wouldn't talk about Miz Gibson until they finished their chores, and to Laura they took forever.

The girls stopped in the barn to get the wheelbarrow, a rake, a shovel, and a garden trowel. Next stop was the manure pile where they filled the wheelbarrow and stacked the tools on top.

"You said you'd tell me about Miz Gibson's music today," Laura said. "I waited all night."

"I'll tell you, but we can't just stand around talking. Pa's done plowed the plants under, and now we got to spread manure and work it in. Your job is to rake it smooth as you can and help me watch Bonnie." Ruth dumped a wheelbarrow full of manure into the garden area, close to where several piles already waited.

"Bonnie and me are ready," Laura said, looking at her baby sister holding the garden trowel in her chubby hands.

"Bonnie, watch what you're doin'. You can help spread the manure, but don't go flippin' it ever'where," Ruth said, as two-year-old Bonnie's enthusiastic shoveling created a cloud of manure all around them. Ruth shook her head at Bonnie's efforts and started turning the garden dirt over to mix the fertilizer in. "Well, first of all, Miz Gibson will play piano more and more as winter sets in. Whenever it's too cold or wet to go outside during the day, she likes to play songs and music games for recess. You'll be clappin' and stompin' to some songs and marching around the room to others. It's lots of fun, and nobody minds being stuck inside when she plays."

"I can't wait." Laura struggled with the rake as she tried to smooth out the ground Ruth had just turned over. The handle was taller than she was, making it awkward to control. "I hope it rains and snows every single day."

"Well, don't get too excited," Ruth answered with a smile. "You know Pa don't believe in using the wagon to take you to school, so when it's rainin' or snowin' in the morning, you'll have to stay home. Most likely you'll only get the music games when it's real cold, or you get surprised by a storm."

Ruth stopped to rest against the shovel a moment. "And you won't like those days when you're walking home, cold and wet through. Those walks seem like forever, when all you want is to get home, strip off your wet clothes and boots, and warm up by the fire." "I won't care if I'm freezin' and wet when I get home, not if Miz Gibson played music at school,"

Laura answered. "If I was Miz Gibson, I'd stay at school all the time just to play that piano."

"She doesn't have to stay at school to play," Ruth said. "Miz Gibson has a piano at her house, and she plays the piano in church every Sunday for services, and at weddings and such."

"In church?" Laura interrupted. "I've never seen her play at church."

"Every Sunday. Can't remember her missin' a single time. You haven't seen her because she's sittin' behind the piano, silly. Only the choir and the preacher can see her."

Laura thought hard. "You're right. We always just see the back of the piano."

"It's her, and she teaches piano lessons at her house, too."

"Piano lessons?" Laura squeaked. "Piano lessons?

Who does she teach?"

"Mostly people in town," Ruth said. "Lessons cost money. Don't know no farmin' family could afford to pay for somethin' like piano lessons."

Little Bonnie dropped the trowel and picked up her doll instead. Ruth and Laura looked at each other and smiled. Laura was glad Bonnie had quit helping. She didn't need Bonnie throwin' manure all over them anymore.

Laura and Ruth continued chatting and working, but Laura lagged behind in spite of her best efforts to keep up with Ruth. So when Ruth told her it was time to go back to the house to start supper, Laura was happy to comply. Leaving the tools in the garden for later, Ruth picked up Bonnie and her doll, then led the way to the house. The door was open, but the air inside was still hot and musty.

"I'm goin' to the root cellar for sweet potatoes and some of those green beans Ma put up," Ruth said, putting the little girl down. "Keep an eye on Bonnie for me."

Laura nodded, and sat on the ground with Bonnie and her doll, thinking hard about what she'd just learned from Ruth.

She was goin' to have a piano in her house someday. She'd be able to play anytime she wanted. All kinds of songs. People would laugh and sing and dance to her music. "Someday," Laura said under her breath, "I'm gonna learn to play piano. I'll play even better'n Miz Gibson."

CHAPTER NINE

Iron Fist

"Those clouds are pretty ugly, but don't look like rain for a few hours, anyway," Ruth said, studying the sky as the youngsters stood in the doorway. "If you don't dawdle on the way to school, you should be fine."

"Aww, Ruth," Ben whined, "them clouds are goin' to rain something fierce, later. We should just stay home."

"No, Ben, you're goin' to school," Ruth said. "Wear your coat, but you're not stayin' home."

The children, bundled up in old wool coats, stayed dry on the way to school, but within an hour of their arrival, the rain engulfed the schoolhouse, pounding against the roof and windows as though a bucket was upended over the building with a never-ending stream. The wood stove kept the room warm, causing the windows to steam up, transforming the class into a cozy cave. The children rushed through dinner at their desks, eager to play with the toys Miz Gibson had placed on the shelves for them, including a box of wooden tops, several yo-yos, two checker games, two sets of tin-can stilts, and a small collection of dolls.

Laura gravitated toward the piano as soon as she finished eating. A quick glance confirmed no one was watching. Unable to resist, she climbed up on the piano bench, her feet almost touching the floor. Laura rubbed her fingers on her skirt, just in case they were sticky or damp, before she touched the keys, caressing the cool surface.

They were so smooth, not like wood at all. The black and white stripes, silky like they'd been polished, and each with its own sound. Laura'd watched Miz Dobbs real close, so she decided she could play, too. With great care, she began to play the ABC song, oblivious to everything around her.

"What d'you think yer doing?" Ben hissed

in Laura's ear. "Get off from there." He grabbed her arm and yanked her off the bench. "Wait till I tell Pa. You'll get a lickin' for sure."

Laura landed on the floor. She cried out in pain as Ben pinched and twisted the muscles of her arm. She tried to get away, but he shoved her back down, straddling her stomach, his knees pinning her arms to the floor.

"Ben," Miz Gibson said, surprising both of them, "Let your sister up, right now. You're hurting her."

"This ain't nothing compared to what Pa will do to her tonight," Ben said, but he got off Laura. His eyes bored into his sister's as he ignored Miz Gibson.

Not in the least impressed, Miz Gibson said, "Ben, you know the rules. You have no right to put your hands on anyone in my classroom. I handle discipline in school, not you."

Miz Gibson paused to help Laura stand up, shaking her head as she looked at the red marks on Laura's arm. "Ben, I'd be more than happy to discuss what happened with your Pa tonight, if you want me to."

Laura watched Ben back away, eyes

wide and mouth agape, staring at Miz Gibson in horror. "No ma'am, no need to do that," Ben said. He shook his head from side to side, a slight tremor in his voice. "I was just tryin' to make sure she didn't hurt the piano." "Alright, then. I appreciate your concern, but it's my job to take care of my students and the piano. If you see someone doing something wrong, you're supposed to tell me, not take action yourself. You may go play with the other boys after you apologize to Laura."

"Sorry." Ben choked, as he walked toward the other side of the room, his face and ears flushed bright red.

Laura realized school was sure different from home. We'd get the belt for tattling if we did what Miz Gibson wants. Now Ben's goin' to blame me for getting him in trouble.

From the look on her brother's face, Laura knew how much he resented being forced to apologize to her, especially in front of other people. When Miz Gibson turned away from both of them and headed back to her desk, Laura watched him glare at the teacher's back, then turn to stare at her.

He shook his fist and mouthed the

words, "I'm gonna get you for this," leaving Laura with no illusions as to what would happen later.

If she told the teacher it was her fault, maybe Miz Gibson'd be nicer to Ben and he might not come after her when they left school.

Laura hurried to Miz Gibson's desk, where the teacher had a stack of slates to correct, each with arithmetic problems from a test she'd given to the older children earlier in the day.

"Excuse me, Miz Gibson," Laura said, her heart pounding. "Ben didn't mean nothin'. No need to talk to our pa. It was my fault anyways. I didn't ask first. And Pa always tells Ben to mind me and our sister Bonnie since he's older."

Laura gazed into Miz Gibson's eyes. It felt like the teacher was looking right inside her head. Could she hear what Laura was thinking? She sure hoped not. They didn't need any more problems at home.

"That's right, Laura, you should have asked to play the piano first. But Ben still had no right to do what he did and has to learn proper manners in my classroom."

Laura listened to Miz Gibson's words, but couldn't help glancing back at the piano.

Miz Gibson smiled when Laura turned back to her. "We still have a little time before class starts, so you can play if you wish."

Hardly believing her good luck, Laura ran to the piano and climbed on the bench. She spread her fingers on the keys and began to play, ignoring her pounding heart. She knew there still might be trouble from Ben, but she no longer cared.

Hours later, walking home in the heavy rain seemed to take forever. Wet and cold, the children walked as fast as they could, heads hunched between their shoulders, their ill-fitting wool coats sodden and heavy.

"I'm goin' to sit right next to the fire when we get home," Laura said. "I'm so cold, I don't know if I'll ever warm up again."

"You won't be sittin' long," Becca responded. "Look how dark it is already. Pa'll be home early 'cause of the rain, and Ruth'll be fixin' supper while there's still light out."

When the house came into view, everyone broke into a shambling trot. Ruth stood just inside the open door waiting for them.

"Don't move away from this door, Laura," Ruth said, as Laura tried to step around her. "All of you get out of those wet coats and boots. Hang the coats up, then stuff some rags in them boots afore you put 'em on the hearth to dry."

"I know, I know," Laura grumbled, as she stood on tiptoes to reach a hook for her coat. She sat as close to the fire as she could, then started stuffing her wet boots.

Laura's skin had just begun to warm, when Ruth said, "That's enough sittin'. Help me get supper on the table," as she shooed Ben and the girls away from the hearth. "Pa's getting the stock bedded down and fed, then he'll be comin' in. I want everything ready for him."

Laura heard Pa muttering to himself as he scraped the mud off his boots just outside the door. The words weren't clear, but the tone of his voice didn't sound good.

"Pa's comin'. He'll be here in just a minute," Lizbeth said, as she carried a pitcher of milk to the table.

"Pa, do you need any help in the barn tonight?" Ben said as Pa came through the door.

"No, ever'thin's done for the night. You can help me tomorrow with some harness repairs. Looks like it'll rain all day," Pa said, sitting down at the table.

Ruth brought a platter of ham, surrounded by potatoes and carrots, to the table and placed it in front of him. Everyone sat down, waiting for Pa to fill his plate first, so they could have their turns.

"I hope it's clear in the morning, so we can go to school." Laura spoke without thinking, catching Ruth's wide eyes just before Pa exploded.

"School? I'm sick a hearin' about school. All a'you better start thinkin' more about what needs doin' around this here farm than wastin' time in school. I checked the root cellar 'fore coming' in, and we're gonna be lucky to have enough food, candles, soap, and other things to get us through to spring." Pa directed his tirade first at Laura, then shifted his gaze to Ruth.

"Looks like you hardly put anythin' away from last summer. Most everythin' on the shelves is from your Ma's work," Pa said, pointing his fork at Ruth. "She should'a spent more time teaching you and your sisters how to take care of a household, 'stead of filling your heads with foolish ideas about schoolin'."

"I'm sorry, Pa, I'll do better this summer, I promise," Ruth said.

Laura watched Ruth look down after she spoke. Ruth loved school. Why was she sayin' that? Oh, Oh, bet she's just tryin' not to make Pa madder than he already was.

Bonnie spoke up. "I wanna go to school. Wanna play the piano, too. Wanna play piano all day when I grow up."

"Piano?" Pa roared. "Piano don't put food on the table or clothes on your backs. You'd all best be thinking' about how to keep this farm goin', 'stead of foolishness."

"Pa, Laura's been tellin' Bonnie all about the piano at school," Ben chimed in, glancing at Laura with a sly smile. "Laura played piano today during dinner recess, without even asking Miz Gibson first."

"Miz Gibson wasn't mad at Laura," Becca said. "She yelled at you 'cause you pulled her off the bench and bruised her arm."

"That's enough." Pa's hand slammed down on the table. causing everyone to jump. "Don't want to hear 'nother word about school. I tol' you before, all the schoolin' you need is how to read, sign your name, and do your sums. Your ma put this nonsense in your heads, but that's over now."

Laura saw the fear on each child's face as Pa turned his attention to them, one by one, around the table. "Ruth, as soon as I can find a woman willin' to teach you, you're going to start learnin' more about woman's work. Your ma should'a taught you, but that can't be helped now. Lizbeth, you've learned enough at school and need to start helpin' Ruth. You're done with schoolin'."

Laura saw Lizbeth's face turn white as she looked from Pa to Ruth. She didn't say a word, but the pleading expression in her eyes was clear. Ruth's quick head-shake in her direction dashed Lizbeth's hope, causing a silent torrent of tears.

"Stop that cryin', girl," Pa said. "You'll do what I tell you, so don't go lookin' at your sister for help."

Pa stared at Becca, then Ben, and lastly at Laura. "You three will still go to school, 'cept when the weather's bad or when you're needed at home, but you've got to do a lot more to help around here. An' I don't want to hear anymore foolishness about playing the piano or other highfalutin ideas from that teacher, you hear, Laura."

"Yes, Pa." Laura replied. Becca and Ben just nodded, then lowered their eyes in silence.

Laura's thoughts weren't quite as obedient as her words. Laura kept her face expressionless, but her thoughts weren't. She was goin' to learn to play music on that piano.

CHAPTER TEN

Magic

August 1911, three years later

Pa followed through with his plans for the children. Lizbeth never went to school again. She stayed at Ruth's side each day, helping with chores and watching the younger ones.

Within a week of his announcement at supper, Pa arranged for Ruth to work with Miz O'Donnell several days a week. Miz O'Donnell, mother of four boys who spent all their time working with their father on their farm, agreed to teach Ruth the fine points of woman's work, such as sewing, gardening, and cooking, in exchange for Ruth's free labor.

Pa felt he'd made a good bargain, but the youngsters hated the change. Ruth did her best to learn from Miz O'Donnell, but found the woman humorless and critical, so different as a teacher from her ma.

Lizbeth and the other girls were miserable on the days Ruth worked with Miz O'Donnell. Lizbeth wasn't able to control the children. In fact, they ignored her and only did the chores assigned to them by Ruth the night before. No matter how hard she tried, Lizbeth could never get her chores done before Pa came home. He had to pick up Ruth at Miz O'Donnell's first, so was always irritated when they arrived. Pa yelled at Lizbeth when supper wasn't ready, then Lizbeth would cry, making Pa even madder. Ruth always finished whatever Lizbeth hadn't done during the day, trying to protect Lizbeth from Pa's temper. The younger girls did their best to stay out of the way.

For two long years the pattern continued until Pa decided Ruth had learned enough and could manage the house on her own. Ruth was just sixteen but accepted her responsibilities as woman of the house and mother to her sisters and brother.

"Laura, I need your help today," Ruth said. "I've got to go to town. Pa gave me a list

of supplies we need, and nobody else is goin'."
Ruth looked around the breakfast table at
Lizbeth, Becca, and Bonnie. "All a'you have
weedin' to do in the garden today, and there'd
better not be any slackin' off. Pa and Ben are
already out in the fields, but if they need
something 'afore I get back, you three will
have to do it."

"I'm ready to go," Laura said. "Never
been inside the store before. I can help you
find things."

"No, you're not," Ruth frowned. "You
look a right mess. Go wash your face and
hands and let's get that hair brushed and
braided. Bad enough putting up with snooty
townsfolk without you shamin' the family
lookin' like you just crawled out of bed."

Laura ran outside to the bucket and
washed her face as fast as she could so Ruth
wouldn't change her mind. Then, as she
walked back inside, she untied the ribbons that
secured her braids and ran her fingers through
the plaits to separate the messy strands. She
grabbed Ma's hairbrush and started working
on the tangles.

"Give me that brush," Ruth said. "You'll
pull out half your hair yankin' at it that way. Sit

down here and I'll help you."

Laura sat on the bench and tipped her head forward. Ruth stood behind her and started brushing. "Tol' you' before, if your hair's all tangled, you have to brush from the bottom up, or it just gets worse."

It didn't take long for Laura's hair to be back in tight, neat braids with ribbon bows securing them in place. Laura turned in a circle in front of her sister to make sure she looked presentable. Then the two headed to the barn to get the horse and wagon.

After Ruth finished harnessing Star, their bay mare, Laura climbed up on the wagon bench next to Ruth.

"Never sat up front on the driver's bench before," she said. "Can I help hold the reins?"

"No," Ruth said, laughing. "First time up here on the wagon bench, first time with us two on a trip, and then first time in the store. Think that's enough firsts for one day. I'll teach you to drive the horse another time."

Star trotted away from the barn when Ruth slapped the reins on her back. "I can see better from here," Laura said, turning from side to side. "Thank you so much for bringin' me."

"You're welcome. We forgot your birthday, so this can be your special celebration," Ruth smiled at Laura. "Keep that to yourself, though, 'cause we don't need the others gettin' upset or thinkin' I'm givin' you special treatment."

"What are we goin' to do? I mean, don't really matter 'cause it's fun just the two of us, but I was just wondering."

"Well, after we finish getting supplies at the store, we can walk around town some, then eat dinner in the town square. And we can talk about anythin' you want," Ruth said.

Laura couldn't hide her excitement, wiggling on the bench seat. "We can talk about anything?"

Ruth nodded yes.

Laura tilted her head and closed her eyes, thinking hard about what to say.

"Okay, there's somethin' I've been wanting to ask you, but not in front of Pa or the others."

"I understand."

"What's a half-breed? Some of the older boys at school call Ben and me that. Ben always gets mad and sometimes fights 'em, but he won't tell me why."

Ruth sighed, then said, "Half-breed is a bad name for somebody with one white parent and one Indian parent."

"Why would they call us that? Pa always says we're Black Irish, so why would anybody think we were half-breed?" A confused look covered Laura's face.

"Oh, Laura, you were too little when Ma died to know, but she was Indian, full blood Cherokee. Pa hates Indians, so didn't want anybody to know. And no matter what people say, ain't nothin' wrong with bein' half Cherokee. Ma was proud of who she was, but kept quiet because Pa didn't want her to talk or sing Cherokee to us."

"You mean the boys are right?"Laura said, surprised. "I mean when they call us half-breed, they're right?"

"No, they ain't right," Ruth said. "That word is ugly, just a nasty insult makin' fun of people. Ma talked to me some about all this before she got sick. She said people are good or bad because of what they do, and how they treat other folks, not on account of who their parents are. She said it's just plain ignorant and mean to call people names like that."

Laura thought for a moment, then said,

"Maybe you should tell Ben, so he can quit fightin'."

"Sure wish it was that easy, but you know Ben'd tell Pa, and Pa'd be madder than a wet hen. Besides, if Pa said the sky was green, Ben'd fight you if you said it was blue, no matter what his own eyes saw. No good tryin' to convince Ben."

Laura hesitated, then blurted out, "Ruth, Ben's just plain mean. Always pickin' on me and Bonnie. Makes her cry whenever nobody's looking. Even when he gets in trouble with Pa, he's always tellin' lies and hurting us. What's wrong with him?"

"I wish I knew why Ben acts the way he does," Ruth said. "He was such a sweet little baby, but then he changed. Sometimes he was downright hateful to Ma, really hurt her feelin's."

Laura had no more questions, but the sound of Star's easy trot, the creak of the wooden wagon moving over the rutted road, and the huffing sound of the breeze filled the comfortable silence.

"Ruth, look at all the wildflowers," Laura said, pointing to the colorful patches dotting the green around them. "Sure are pretty."

"Yes they are. Ma loved flowers. Always managed to plant some around the edges of the truck garden plots. She said some of them helped keep bugs away, something about how the bugs didn't like the smell of certain plants. Wish I remembered more about which ones she said worked. Miz O'Donnell just made a face when I asked her."

"Would there be time to go see Ma's grave? Maybe take her some flowers?"

Ruth smiled. "That's a fine idea, we'll make time." Ruth pulled the reins back to stop Star. "Let's pick a whole bunch for her."

Soon the wagon had a pile of yellow Goldenrod and Ashy Sunflowers, purple Slender Bush clover, white Snow-on-the-Mountain, Blue Sage, and red Cardinal Flowers in the bed, their spicy fragrance filling the wagon. Ruth covered them with a flour sack, then dampened the material from their water jug to keep the flowers from wilting in the heat.

"Can we have our picnic at Ma's grave?" We could go after we're done at the store and maybe make the flowers into a pretty chain for her."

Ruth turned to Laura and smiled. "That'd

be the perfect end of our day. We'll have to remember to get more water though, cause most of what I brought will go to keeping the flowers fresh."

When they arrived in town, Ruth guided Star to the front of the General Store, positioning the wagon next to the raised sidewalk. Then she jumped down and secured the reins to a convenient hitching rail next to a watering trough.

"Come on, Laura," Ruth said, leading the way. "Time to get those supplies."

A huge smile on her face, Laura jumped down and followed Ruth inside. Ruth walked to the long side of an L-shaped counter, which ran down the middle of the store. The short side faced the door, about ten feet away. Tucked into the corner between the wall and the short counter was a wood stove, unlit on this hot day, with three chairs for customers. Two of the chairs were occupied by men with full gray beards, their attention focused on a chess game between them on top of an empty nail keg.

Ruth was showing her list to a young man at the long counter, so Laura felt free to explore. She was struck by the strong smells that filled the room, even before moving away from the door. She recognized the pungent odor of tobacco juice from the spittoon next to the barrel by the chess players, the rich fragrance of leather coming from deep in the store, and the spicy smell of coffee. Each wall was lined with shelves full of all kinds of goods, above full bins and stacked cloth bags, stuffed tight. She watched two store employees, wearing aprons with the store name sewn on, fetching things from throughout the store for Ruth and another customer standing at the counter.

Laura walked to the left, toward the open aisle next to the wall, examining the clothes piled on the first row of tables, one of several rows between the counter and left wall. Her attention was riveted by stacks of brand new clothes. She touched and stroked the crisp, smooth fabrics. The colors were so pretty and bright. She'd never had any new things from a store. Ruth most always made new things for Ben or herself since there weren't so many hand-me-downs for them. Most ever'thing she'd ever had was patched and passed down. Someday I'd like to have me a store-bought dress that nobody else'd ever worn.

The side wall shelves were weighted down with what seemed like incredible riches. Everything Laura could think of was on display, all new and shiny. Dishes in many colors and pretty patterns, pots, pans, basins and tubs of every possible size and shape, utensils made of tin as well as silver, store-bought soaps smelling like flowers and spices, washboards, ropes, and tools of all types and sizes filled every inch of the shelves. Underneath the shelving, bins filled with shiny new nails and screws filled half the wall, next to cloth bags filled with flour, sugar, salt, cornmeal, beans, lentils, and all kinds of seeds.

Laura couldn't believe the store could have so many different things. She moved down the long aisle, touching things as she passed each display. And there were sewing things. She stopped at one of the tables, feasting her eyes on bolts of cloth, skeins of yarn, crochet hooks and knitting needles, together with spools of thread piled high near some scissors and packets of sewing needles.

Tearing herself away from the tables, Laura resumed walking down the aisle, then stopped short when the bright covers on a rack of paper-back books caught her attention.

They even sold books? Laura wished she could buy 'em all, then hide in the barn and read all day. Laura stood there, reading as many of the titles as she could until she heard Ruth calling her.

"Sorry, I didn't hear you callin' at first," Laura said, hurrying to Ruth's side. "There's a whole bunch of books back there."

Ruth laughed. "I know, but those books are not for children. I hope you didn't open them."

"Course not, don't belong to me," she replied, looking up at her sister. Then she caught sight of two big glass jars on top of the long counter, near the cash register. One was filled with what looked like brilliant round jewels in all the colors of the rainbow. The other had sticks with shiny blue, red and green stripes twisting around them from top to bottom.

"Oh, my goodness, Ruth, look at those," she whispered, her mouth watering as she imagined how the beautiful candies would taste.

"Pretty, aren't they," Ruth said. "But we can't afford store-bought candy."

"What color would you like? Every pretty

little girl should get to choose one special candy for herself. My treat," the smiling young man behind the counter said, gesturing to the beautiful jars.

"No thank you, Paul. Pa would have a fit if we accepted charity," Ruth said. "It's nice of you to offer, but we can't. Laura, go on out to the wagon. I'll be there in a minute."

Laura's excitement at the opportunity to make such an incredible choice, ended. Ruth's voice made it clear there would be no discussion. "Yes, ma'am." She sighed, her shoulders drooping as she left the store.

When the wagon was filled with their purchases, and more water had been poured over the cloth covered flowers which Laura had moved to the back of the wagon bed, Ruth headed for the church. Ma's grave was at the very back of the cemetery, with plenty of room nearby for the wagon and lots of grass for the patient mare to graze on.

"Get the blanket and dinner basket while I unhook Star," Ruth said.

Laura climbed down and walked to the plain wooden cross marking Ma's grave. She stared at the words carved into the simple marker.

Vera Cavanaugh 1876 – 1907

The wood was weathered to a silvery color, and the carved letters were no longer easy to read against the smooth surface of the crossbeam.

"Give me the blanket," Ruth tugged the material free from Laura's arms, "and we'll get settled for our picnic."

"I'll get the flowers," Laura said, "They'll make a real pretty chain for Ma."

The sisters sat cross-legged on the blanket, flowers heaped between them, as they ate. As soon as they finished, Laura and Ruth began plaiting stems together.

"I miss Ma so much," she whispered, surprised to feel tears filling her eyes. "But I can't remember her face."

"I miss her, too," Ruth said. "Not surprised you don't remember much, you were just three when she passed. Poor Bonnie was so little, she won't remember Ma at all."

"I remember sittin' in her lap in the rocker. She was warm, and her arms felt good around me. Sometimes she'd hum while we rocked." The tears ran down

Laura's face, dropping onto her hands as she worked on the flower chain.

"Ma hummed because Pa got mad whenever she sang to us. Her songs were Cherokee, and he hated her singing 'em." Ruth said.

"I just wish I could remember how she looked," Laura said. "She was pretty, wasn't she?"

"Very pretty," Ruth said, looking at Laura's face. "I think you favor Ma more than any of us."

"Really?" Laura was surprised, but pleased.

"Yep, your hair is black like hers instead of brown like Pa's, and straighter than the rest of us." Ruth studied Laura's features. "And your skin's a little darker. Looks like your cheekbones are sharper too, more like Ma's."

"I'd like that. If I look kinda like Ma, maybe I can remember her better." Laura wiped her tears away and smiled. "Chain's done. Let's see how it looks."

Ruth hung the flowers from the crossbar, then both stepped back to study the result. The bright colors of the flowers, entwined with the different shades of green stems braided together, framed the letters in graceful loops and scented the air with their sweet perfume.

"If Ma was born in eighteen-seventy-six and died in nineteen-ought-seven, she was thirty-one when she died, right?" Laura traced the letters carved into the wood.

"That's right." Ruth hugged her sister close. "Good job doing the 'rithmetic."

"Is that old? It sounds kinda' old, but I don't remember Ma bein' old like Miz Gibson or Miz Dobbs."

"Ma was younger than them. Just wish we'd had her longer," Ruth said. "Come on, now, we need to get home before Pa does."

Hand in hand, the sisters strolled to the wagon. A few minutes after they were on the way home, Laura turned to Ruth and said, "Can I ask you something?"

"Sure, what do you want to know?" Ruth held the reins loosely, her attention on Laura.

"Not really a question, just something I need to tell you," Laura began. "When I'm feelin' bad, I think about Ma and get to missing her somethin' fierce."

"Me, too, honey. Me too."

"When I'm really down, or Pa's been 'specially mean, sometimes I hear her humming. Not out loud, of course, 'cause I know she's gone, but I hear the sound of her humming kind of inside my head." Laura looked at Ruth, not sure of how her confession would be received.

"Oh, Laura," Ruth said, "we all miss Ma and think about her. And when we think about her we remember lots of things about her. Not surprisin' you'd think of her humming when you need some comfort."

"No, Ruth, I'm not thinking about her," Laura insisted. "I hear her hummin' to me all of a sudden. I never know when it'll happen or how long it'll last. One time I even thought I heard her say my name."

Ruth sighed, took a deep breath, then said, "I know it must seem real, but nobody can hear the dead talking or hummin'. Your mind is making up things. You know Ma is not coming to you, and you need to stop thinking it's real. Just remember Ma's dead and can't come back no matter how much you want her to."

Laura didn't say another word about Ma

on the way home, only speaking when Ruth
asked her a question or they made small talk.
She preferred silence as she listened to Ma's
voice humming in her mind, then the soft
words of a song she remembered Ma singing
to Bonnie to calm her when Pa was away.

We N' De Ya Ho, WeN' De Ya Ho
We N' De Ya, We N' De Ya
Ho, Ho Ho Ho
He Ya Ho, He Ya Ho
Ya Ya Yaaa

The melody was haunting, and the soft,
sweet sound of the words warmed Laura and
filled her with peace. How can it be my
imagination when I never knew the words?
Laura smiled, thankful for her special gift
from Ma.

CHAPTER ELEVEN

Collision Course

September 1914, three years later

R uth filled her role as the center of the family so well that the children, except for Ben, accepted her authority without question.

Once Ruth stopped spending days at Miz O'Donnell's place, she started teaching Lizbeth what she'd learned.

Pa was the undisputed master of the household, however, and overruled Ruth's attempts to keep Becca in school. When Becca begged to quit and spend her days with Lizbeth and Ruth, she had no trouble convincing Pa to let her stop. Lizbeth and Becca had always been close, and once Becca was home each day, the three sisters handled all the farm chores much faster than anyone could alone.

Ruth made most of the trips into town when Pa needed supplies, sometimes taking one of the other youngsters to help. She watched the town double in size after a train station was built, creating more demand for farm products like eggs, butter and fresh produce. Ruth, together with Lizbeth and Becca, talked to Pa about selling eggs and butter to the General Store. He'd agreed and made arrangements for Ruth to deposit the earnings into his account at the town bank. Within just a few months, Ruth was making trips to the store every week. In two years, the earnings from eggs and butter had become a substantial income producer for the family.

Laura and Bonnie, the only ones in the family still attending school, found Lizbeth and Becca sitting outside the open door shelling peas when they got home. Glancing inside, Laura was surprised to see the house was empty.

"Where's Ruth?" she asked, "Gonna be a sad supper if you two are fixin' it by yourselves."

"She was cryin' when she got home from town," Lizbeth said. "Told us to get supper tonight, then ran out toward the garden."

"What happened?" Laura asked.

"Don't rightly know. She just left after tellin' us to stay here," Becca said.

"Bonnie, you stay and help with supper. I'll go find out what's goin' on," Laura said, then headed toward the garden.

"God, I hate him, I hate him, I hate him."

Laura heard Ruth before she found her hidden between rows of corn, sitting on an overturned metal tub. She was rocking back and forth, fists pounding her thighs in time to the words, "I hate him, I hate him."

"What happened? What's wrong?" Laura knelt down in front of Ruth so they were face to face.

"I was in the store getting supplies. I didn't know that Pa and Ben were at the blacksmith getting two horses shod. Guess Ben got bored waitin', and went walkin' around. He looked into the window of the store and saw me talking to Paul." Ruth dried her tears with her sleeve and continued. "We weren't doing nothin', just talking. Don't know what Ben told Pa, but when I came out, Pa was standin' there waitin' for me. He slapped me across the face and knocked me down, right there in public. He called me a whore and ordered me home."

Laura wrapped her arms around Ruth, hugging and rocking her as Ruth's tears fell. "I hate him too," Laura said. "It's not fair he's still here, mean as a snake, and Ma gone instead."

They tensed with fear when they heard galloping horses, knowing Pa and Ben had arrived home. "Don't hide from me, you whore. I'm not done with you, yet," Pa roared, the venom in his voice clear even at a distance.

Ruth jumped to her feet, her fists clenched, then turned toward Pa's voice, ready to defend herself. "Laura, get away from me or you might get hurt. You need to go back to the house."

"No, Ruth, no tellin' what he'll do." Laura clung to Ruth's arm. "I can't just let him hurt you when you didn't do nothin' wrong."

"Get out of sight, at least, before he gets here." Ruth pushed Laura away toward the tall stalks, begging her to hide.

"There you are, you worthless slut," Pa looked murderous, with the tendons in his neck standing out in sharp relief below his clenched jaw and slitted eyes. He was still holding the riding crop in his hand as he strode through the rows toward Ruth.

"Pa, stop it. I didn't do nothin' wrong. You had no call to slap me, like you did, right in front of ever'body in town, treatin' me worse than a dog."

Laura could see that Ruth was afraid but determined to stand and defend herself. She couldn't let him hurt Ruth just 'cause Ben lied.

"Nothing wrong? Flirtin' with that boy like a common harlot? Shamin' me in public with your whorin' ways?" Pa's voice was pitched low and fierce with rage. He raised the short whip, the handle still looped around his right fist, and struck Ruth across her shoulders.

Ruth screamed, spun around by the blow. "Stop it, Pa, You're wrong. You shamed yourself actin' crazy, yellin' and hittin' me in front of ever'body."

Pa, infuriated even further by her words, raised the whip again. Before he could strike, Laura, screaming, leaped on his arm, and stopped him from striking Ruth.

"Leave her alone," Laura shrieked,

hanging on to his arm with all her strength, determined to defend Ruth no matter what.

"You little bitch." Pa shoved Laura away as hard as he could. "I swear I'll beat both a you to death if I want to. You're just like your ma, nothing but injun whores."

This time, without Laura to interfere with his swing, the whip hit Ruth hard, cutting into her flesh. Laura landed on her back, unable to stand or even take a breath, much less help her sister. The whip landed two more times before Laura could get up, "Stop it, Pa, stop it," she screamed as the leather whistled through the air with each strike, her voice full of anger at Pa, and terror for Ruth.

"Laura, run. Please get back to the house 'fore he hurts you bad," Ruth cried out, trying to dodge the blows of the whip. "Please, Laura, I promise I'll be alright."

Not knowing what to do, and afraid that she'd only make it worse for her sister, Laura turned and stumbled back toward the house, feeling like a coward. Maybe Pa'd stop hittin' Ruth with her gone. Maybe Lizbeth and Becca would help stop him.

With Ruth's cries ringing in Laura's ears, she ran. When the front of the house came into view, she saw Ben glance back at her from just outside the front door, then sprint toward the barn.

Once inside, Laura tried to get Lizbeth or Becca to help her, but they both just shook their heads. Defeated, Laura sank down to the floor. "Oh Ruth, I'm so sorry." Laura said aloud as she huddled in a corner, shaking and crying. She'd promised to get help, but ever'body was too afraid of Pa to do anything. "Please, please." Laura held her hands and prayed out loud, "Please. she has to be alright."

Laura was still in the corner, with her head on her knees and her arms wrapped around her body, when Pa came into the house.

"Not one word from any a you." Pa was breathing hard, his big hands covered with dirt and blood, his body stinking of sweat. "All of you best learn to obey me, or I'll beat you like a dog iffen that's what it takes. I'm goin' to get cleaned up, then supper better be on the table, with ever'one a you in your places with your mouths shut."

No one made a sound during the meal. Glancing at her sisters, Laura saw that they were too terrified to even look at Pa. She hoped they'd stay quiet and not draw his attention. Laura was frozen with fear for Ruth, who never appeared at the table.

Laura waited until everything was cleaned up after supper and the pallets were rolled out. Then a little longer until Pa started snoring. When she was confident that everyone was asleep, Laura sneaked out the door to find Ruth.

Once outside, Laura ran, the light from the moon guiding her steps. She headed toward the garden where she'd left Ruth, but stopped when she realized Ruth would have sought a hiding place where she could rest out of the cold air.

The barn. I'll bet Ruth went to the barn where she'd be warm and safe. Oh, please let her be alright. Laura prayed hard as she changed directions and ran for the barn as fast as she could.

Trying not to make a sound, Laura slipped through the barn door. "Ruth, Ruth, where are you?"

"You shouldn't be here." Ruth's weak voice led Laura deep inside the barn to one of the empty stalls.

"Are you okay?" Laura rushed to Ruth's side and knelt down next to her. She was resting on a pile of hay in the corner of the stall, covered by an old, dirty horse blanket. Ruth tried to sit up, but her slow movements, together with a hiss of pain, tore at Laura's heart. "How bad are you hurt? What can I do? We've got to

get you some help."

"My back's on fire, and I can feel blood drippin' down." Ruth grabbed Laura's hands. "I'm never going' back in that house again as long as he's there. I mean it, he's never, ever goin' to hit me again." Ruth squeezed Laura's hands hard as she spoke. "I need to get to Miz Dobbs. Can you help me on the mule?"

Without the slightest hesitation, Laura agreed, and moved away to the mule's stall. "Easy, Daisy. Sorry to wake you up, girl, but you've got to stay quiet and help us." In minutes, she slipped a halter over the sleepy animal's head, then tightened a saddle blanket over her back. That done, Laura led the mule to where Ruth waited.

Ruth wasn't able to mount the mule by herself. She held on to the stall door, then stepped up on a wooden box to reach the mule's back, but needed Laura's support to climb on since she was too weak to ride alone. Laura took Daisy out of the barn, closed the door behind them, then climbed up in front of Ruth. Daisy started trotting toward Miz Dobb's place after Laura kicked her sides a few times to get her going.

Determined to secure Miz Dobbs' healing services for her sister, Laura rode the mule as fast as they dared in the moonlight. Ruth's body was heavy and awkward against her sister's back. Her arms were wrapped tight around Laura's waist, making it difficult to breathe. She found it hard to ride supporting her sister's weight on her back, but the pressure of Ruth's arms assured Laura that she was still conscious.

Laura was thankful the moon was bright, so she could see the road. She hoped Miz Dobbs was home and not out helping birth a baby somewheres. Laura whispered, "She has to fix Ruth, she just has to."

"There's her place. Just a few more minutes," Laura said, when Miz Dobbs house came into view. "Not long now." Ruth didn't say a word, but Laura felt her nod her head.

Laura stopped Daisy in the yard, hoping

someone was inside the dark building. "Hold on while I slide off, then I can help you down."

Ruth fell, rather than dismounted, crying out as she landed against her little sister. Laura reached around Ruth's waist to help her walk, horrified at the wetness that soaked the back of Ruth's torn dress. Together they walked to the door. Laura knocked as hard as she could.

"Miz Dobbs," Laura called, "Please help us. My sister Ruth is hurt real bad."

"Quit bangin' on the door, girl. I'm comin' fast as I can." Miz Dobbs sounded sleepy, but soon opened the door. "What's goin' on?"

"Please, Miz Dobbs," Laura said. "Pa hurt Ruth bad. Her back's all cut up from where he hit her with a horsewhip."

Miz Dobbs reached out for Ruth, and, with Laura's help, walked her into the house. When they moved into the lantern light, Miz Dobbs looked at the cuts that ribboned the fabric covering Ruth's back. "Lord a'mercy. Hold on, honey," Miz Dobbs whispered to Ruth. "I'll take care a you."

"Laura, I need you to hold Ruth steady while I put blankets on the table for her," Miz

Dobbs said, then disappeared into the curtained off bedroom area where her husband waited. After a whispered conversation, she came back out and spread blankets on the table.

"You're safe now," Miz Dobbs guided Ruth to the table and helped her stretch out on her stomach. "I've got to get some hot water to clean your wounds. Just rest. No need to worry." Miz Dobbs lit the woodstove and started heating a pot of water, then led Laura outside and demanded an explanation.

Laura told her the story. "Ben told Pa that Ruth was flirtin' with a boy in town, so Pa slapped her and called her awful names. She came home cryin', and told me it wasn't true. When Pa got home, he was madder than ever and took after her with the ridin' crop, just kept hittin' her and hittin' her." Laura was crying hard when she finished. "Please help her, Miz Dobbs. Ruth said she never wants to come home, and that she won't ever let Pa hit her again."

Miz Dobbs gave Laura a fierce hug, then said, "Don't you worry 'bout your sister. I'll take care of her back, then we'll figure out what to do next. And iffen your pa comes here after her, my William will protect her."

"Thank you," Laura said. "Thank you so much." "You're welcome, but you better be gettin' on home 'fore your Pa wakes up," Miz Dobbs said. "Wait a minute. We gotta wash that blood off you first. Don't want him to know you helped Ruth get away."

Miz Dobbs was right. Laura's sleeves and hands were covered in blood. Laura washed with care, trying to make sure she got every spot, and wrung her sleeves as dry as she could. Then Laura left the house and rode Daisy home as fast as they dared in the dark. She settled the tired mule back into her stall, put the tack away, then left the barn and sneaked back into the house.

"Thank goodness." Laura whispered under her breath as she tiptoed inside and saw that everybody was sleeping.

Laura stretched out on her pallet and closed her eyes, but couldn't get Ruth out of her mind. Ma, if you're out there somewhere, please watch over Ruth. She's just gotta be alright.

CHAPTER TWELVE

Turmoil to Triumph

L izbeth," Pa's loud voice woke Laura with a start, "Lizbeth, get up. Your lazy whore sister done run off, so you need to start fixin' breakfast and packin' dinner pails."

Lizbeth got up, followed by Becca. Neither said a word, but working as a team they got the woodstove started and brought in water for coffee and grits. Then Becca started beating eggs for scrambling while Lizbeth sliced pieces of ham. Only when Ben stopped watching them and went outside, did Lizbeth turn to Laura. "What did Pa mean when he said Ruth done run off? You saw her last. What happened?" Lizbeth whispered.

"Don't know," Laura said, trying to keep her voice low so Bonnie, who was sitting up on her pallet, yawning and rubbing sleep out of her eyes, wouldn't hear. "When she made me leave, Pa was yellin' and hittin' her with the whip. Didn't want to leave her, but she told me to. That's all I know."

Laura saw the look that passed between her sisters and knew they didn't believe her. She had to get away before she said something wrong. She needed to check the barn and make sure she hadn't left something there. Laura didn't dare go now. She'd have to try after Pa and Ben came in to eat.

"Come on, Bonnie," Laura said, grabbing her sister's hand, "Let's get washed up before Pa and Ben get back. Then I'll help you brush your hair for school."

Pa and Ben came inside after they'd fed the stock, milked the cows, and brought the cans of fresh milk to the house to be run through the cream separator. They found four lard cans packed with dinner on the counter, and Lizbeth and Becca placing steaming food on the table. As usual, there was no conversation at the table while the family ate their breakfast. Pa and Ben were served first and left the house as soon as they finished eating.

Laura ate as fast as she could. After Pa and Ben were gone, she said, "Becca, you're helping Lizbeth, so I'll go bring in the eggs." Before anyone could say a word, she left the house, heading for the chicken coop. Laura scooped eggs from under the disgruntled hens much faster than usual, placed the full egg basket next to the coop door, then headed for the barn.

If anyone saw her, she'd just say she was going for more feed. Ruth usually took care of the chickens, so I'm just makin' sure the birds get fed.

Laura knew Pa would come to the barn soon to get the horses ready, so she raced to Daisy's stall. Seeing nothing suspicious, she checked the mule's tack, then ran to the stall where she'd found Ruth curled up in the hay. The blanket was still crumpled in the same place, so she picked it up, folded it in half, and put it back in the trunk where horse blankets were stored. There were bloodstains in the straw, so she added more hay on top to cover them up.

Laura was just leaving the barn with a bucket full of feed when Pa came in. Stepping around him, not daring to breath until she heard him move deeper into the barn, she walked to the chicken coop. Laura found Lizbeth waiting for her, just inside the closed coop door.

The two sisters didn't move until they saw Pa and Ben leave, Pa in the wagon and Ben on horseback. Then Lizbeth grabbed Laura's arm and said, "Tell me where Ruth is. We all heard her screamin' last night. What happened?"

"You can't tell Becca or Bonnie. You know they can't keep a secret from Pa," Laura said.

"Why do you think I came out here? Becca's keepin' Bonnie busy, so's we can talk in private," Lizbeth said. "Did Ruth really run away?"

"She was hurt so bad she couldn't have run any-where," Laura said, then ran through the story while keeping one eye on the house, not wanting to be caught by Becca or Bonnie. "I had to help her, no way Ruth could have walked away on her own, and I was afraid she'd die all by herself."

Lizbeth stepped back, eyes wide, and gasped. "If Pa finds out you helped, he'll beat you worse'n he did Ruth."

"I know, so he can't find out. And that means we can't let anyone else know. Miz Dobbs promised she wouldn't tell, and she was real mad about how bad Pa hurt Ruth. She said if Pa showed up, Mr. Dobbs wouldn't let him near her."

"But Laura," Lizbeth said, "what'll happen when Ruth's better? Pa'll blame her for shamin' him to Miz Dobbs and go after her again."

Laura shook her head no, "Ruth won't ever be back here. Don't know where she'll go, but she kept sayin' she'd never, ever let Pa hit her again. And I believe she meant it."

Laura saw Bonnie come out of the house, headed toward the chicken coop. "Whatever you do, don't tell Becca or Bonnie. Goin' to be hard on you, 'cause you're the oldest now, but Becca will help. I'll do what I can and try to take care of Bonnie."

"Don't worry, I'm not tellin' nobody. Just wish I could get away too."

Laura led Lizbeth toward the house, wishing for the same thing.

The next week crawled by for Laura and

Lizbeth. Pa was angry the whole time, but the children stayed out of his way as much as they could, and never talked around him except to respond to a question. Normal routines filled the hours, but Laura's thoughts never strayed far from Ruth.

Was Ruth still with Miz Dobbs? Was her back healing' up? Those cuts looked real bad. They'd be sure to leave marks. Will Miz Dobbs help her get away? Where will she go? The questions circled around in Laura's mind over and over, even invading her dreams.

After another full week, the tension in the house began to ease a little. At supper, Pa looked at Lizbeth and pointed his fork at her. "You haf'ta go to town tomorrow. We got eggs and butter that need to get to the store 'afore they're too old to sell. I've got a list of things for you to buy while you're there."

Laura kept her face expressionless when she heard Pa's words, but she couldn't help but cheer inside. He'd given up on Ruth ever comin' back, otherwise he wouldn't trust Lizbeth to go alone, 'specially to handle the eggs and butter.

Laura had a hard time concentrating in school the next day and hurried Bonnie all the way home.

Laura wondered how Lizbeth did goin' to town. Ruth always said folks in town gossiped all the time and seemed to know ever'body's business. Laura was curious to know if anybody heard about what happened to her.

Becca was sitting outside peeling and cutting potatoes when Laura and Bonnie arrived home. "Laura, Lizbeth wants you to go straight to the root cellar," Becca said. "She says it needs some cleanin' and rearrangin' and wants you to help. Bonnie, you're s'posed to help me get things ready for supper."

Laura nodded, and headed for the cellar, figuring Lizbeth knew somethin'. Leastways, Laura hoped she did. Laura didn't want Becca to get suspicious, so kept her pace at a normal speed.

The minute Laura reached the cellar, Lizbeth pulled her inside by the arm, then shut and barred the door. She picked up a lantern, the only light in the dark, damp interior, and led Laura all the way to the back wall. Lizbeth whispered, "I saw Ruth today."

"You did? Is she alright? Where is she?" The questions poured out of Laura.

"Hush," Lizbeth said. "I'll tell you

ever'thin', but we've got to be careful."

"Sorry. You're right," Laura said.

"When I got to the store, the store owner's son, Paul, was behind the counter. He told me he had to take care of the other two customers first, 'cause it'd take awhile to get what Pa had on his list. Then when they left, he touched my arm, put his finger to his lips, and led me through a door behind the counter. And she was there. Ruth was right at the base of the stairs."

"Oh, my goodness, how did she get there? How did she look? What did she say?"

Lizbeth leaned closer to Laura and told the story. "Ruth stayed at Miz Dobbs' place for three days, so her back could start healin' and she could get some strength back. Mr. and Miz Dobbs were afraid Pa'd come lookin', so they kept her hidden in the bedroom during the day. On the third day Miz Dobbs went into town to get some things, and had a long talk with Miz Carpenter. You know who she is, don't you?"

"Sure, the Carpenters own the store. Paul, the one Ruth was talkin' to, is their boy."

"That's right," Lizbeth said. They don't much like Pa anyways and hated hearin' what he did to Ruth. 'Specially since he was accusing her of bein' unseemly with their son. Ruth said Mr. Carpenter was fit to be tied hearing what Pa said about Paul."

"They're nice folks, and Paul is always polite at the store. He even offered me free candy the first time Ruth took me there," Laura said, smiling at the memory. "But where is Ruth, now?"

"I'm gettin' there," Lizbeth said. "The Carpenters have a spare room upstairs that used to be a storeroom for extra inventory. " They told Miz Dobbs to hide Ruth in the wagon and bring her to town that night. They promised to take care of Ruth as long as she needed their help. She's been hiding there ever since, right above the store. And guess what, since she's nineteen, Pa can't make her come back."

Laura gasped, eyes wide, "Pa'll be ready to beat her all over again for telling on him. Does anyone else but the Carpenters know?"

"Don't think she's shown herself to anyone in town yet, but when she's ready, the Carpenters will let her work for them in the store and keep livin' in their extra room. When Pa finds out, he can't do nothing because he needs to trade with the store, and as long as they're protectin' Ruth and she stays in town, he can't touch her."

"I can't even imagine how mad he'll be," Laura said. "But knowing Pa he'll come up with some story about not wanting her ever coming to the farm again. Just like it's his idea for her to stay away."

Lizbeth nodded in agreement, but her reply was cut off by the sound of the crossbar on the door rattling.

"What's takin' you so long?" Bonnie's voice came from outside, accompanied by the sound of her banging on the door. "Why's the door barred?"

"Sorry, Bonnie," Lizbeth said, opening the door and leading Laura outside to join their baby sister. "Closed it 'cause there was some hornets buzzin' around. Didn't want 'em chasin' us inside."

Laura smiled at Lizbeth's quick thinking and winked at her over Bonnie's head. "We can finish sorting out the old jars in the cellar tomorrow. Let's go help the girls fix supper."

CHAPTER THIRTEEN

Never Again

Ten months later

Lizbeth tried hard to fill Ruth's shoes, but it took both her and Becca to handle all that Ruth used to do. As the weeks and months passed, Pa's attitude and behavior never changed. He yelled at them almost every day, often adding emphasis with a slap to the head, telling them they were useless. Sometimes he'd laugh and say the two of them together weren't worth as much as one good mule.

Lizbeth, always remembering the price Ruth had paid for her defiance, never said a word back. More than once her nails bit into the skin of her palms as she fought to maintain control under his constant bullying. Becca always ended up in tears under Pa's attacks, keeping her eyes down and her sobs silent. The sisters clung to each other for strength, always happiest when Pa was away from the house.

Ben ignored both Lizbeth and Becca when Pa was home, but he always bullied them whenever they were left alone. He bossed Lizbeth and Becca around and repeated every nasty insult he'd heard Pa hurl at them. Ben pulled simple boyish pranks like yanking their hair or tripping them when they walked by. But he also did meaner things like deliberately dumping fresh laundry in the dirt, or knocking over pitchers of water in the house. Causing the girls extra work seemed to delight him, almost as much as making comments or telling stories to get them in trouble with Pa.

Laura spent most of her time working in the garden, almost always with Bonnie in tow. Her biggest job was keeping their youngest sister out of Lizbeth and Becca's way. Laura also tried to keep Bonnie away from Ben. For some reason she couldn't explain, Laura felt uneasy whenever he was around her little sister.

Bonnie adored all her sisters but never seemed able to learn the tasks they tried to teach her. Some of the kids in school teased

Bonnie and made fun of her for being slow. Laura knew there was some truth in their taunts.

Lizbeth and Becca always started the day well before dawn in order to have Pa's breakfast ready. Laura got up with them one morning, much earlier than usual for her. She ate two pieces of bread smeared with butter, drank a glass of water, then headed to the barn carrying a lard can packed with dinner. It would be a long, grueling day away from home, so she'd packed some food to carry her through. The night before, Pa had told Laura to fetch barrels of water from the river and she wanted to get started as early as possible. The cistern was low, and the garden needed water. They didn't dare depend on a convenient rain storm so refilling their stores from the river was a necessity.

The empty wooden barrels were heavy and awkward, but Laura managed to push six of them up into the wagon bed using the back of the wagon as a ramp. She lined the lids up on edge between the barrels and the slats of the wagon sides, then wedged a metal bucket in with the barrels. When everything was in place, Laura secured the ramp back at the rear of the wagon.

After loading the wagon, she harnessed the reluctant horse, petting and soothing Star as she fastened the heavy leather straps. Dawn was just beginning to color the black sky with faint shades of gray when Laura climbed up onto the wagon bench. She slapped the reins on Star's back, urging her forward.

Laura could tell the day would be hot and long since she had already sweated through her dress before they even started. The river was only about six miles from their house, but the flat, grassy plain between the farm and the water provided no respite from the heat. Not even a hint of a breeze stirred the still, heavy air.

"Come on, Star. I'm burning up too, but it'll be cooler by the water." She wiped at her face to get rid of the biting flies attracted by the sweat beading on her skin. She could see dozens of the pesky insects dotting the damp patches that darkened the horse's body and watched Star's tail swishing them away from the wet spots on her sides. "You'll feel better under the trees, 'specially after a cool drink from the river. And hopefully there won't be so many flies, neither."

The wooden barrels and the metal bucket thumped and jiggled against each other as the wagon moved down the bumpy path. After working all day drawing water, she figured it'd probably rain like mad in a day or two.

"I sure miss Ruth," Laura said out loud, knowing Star liked being talked to. "Fetching water was a lot more fun with her. Glad she's safe now, livin' in town above the store. I got to see her room last time Lizbeth took me with her to town. Ruth's room's mighty small, but she's happy."

Laura laughed at her own words, then said, "That's kind of funny, Star, me calling Ruth's room small. At least she has space of her own, even a real bed. No room for more than the bed, a little table with a couple of drawers, and a chair, but still lots better than sleepin' on a pallet in a room with the whole family." Laura watched Star's ears twitch back at the sound of her voice. "Everybody in town knows Ruth's living with the Carpenters. Pa told his drinkin' buddies at the saloon that he'd thrown her out, but didn't dare say anything more, what with the Carpenter's lookin' out for her. She's goin' to marry Paul soon. His pa was so mad when he heard what Pa did, he wanted to whip him. Don't guess we'll get to see 'em get married though, Pa'd never stand for it."

Laura sighed. "Nothin's the same without Ruth.

Just wish I could get away, too."

Star's pace picked up, and she turned her head, pricking her ears. In minutes a rider appeared, approaching from the side. Laura recognized Ben but hoped he'd just pass them by.

No such luck. "Better hurry up," Ben said when he reached the wagon, riding as close to the left front wheel as he could. "You'll never get that water back 'fore it gets late iffen you keep dawdlin'."

"Don't tell me what to do. I been doin' this job a long time," Laura snapped back, not looking at her brother.

Ben leaned in, yanking Laura's braid for emphasis. "Sassin' me will just get you in trouble. When you gonna learn that men make the rules in our house?"

"Men? You're 15 years old, Ben Cavanaugh, long way from bein' a man." Laura snorted and shook her head. "Men? That's pretty funny. One man and a boy who's nothin' but a bully . . . and a dumb one at that.

Pa told me to get the water, and I'm doin' it. Don't need any help or bossin' from you."

Ben started to say something, but stopped, his face flushed red. He glared at Laura. "You better start respectin' me, or you'll be sorry," His words were loud and harsh.

Laura refused to look as Ben galloped away, her heart racing and her hands trembling on the reins. She shouldn't of said what she did, but Ben made her so mad, takin' on airs the way he did. Even startin' to sound like Pa. Good thing she wouldn't be home for awhile. Hope he doesn't take his mad out on somebody else.

It didn't take long for Laura's wagon to reach the trees near the riverbank. The air felt much cooler in the shade, with the soothing sound of the water flowing. Laura drove Star forward to the edge of the river to make it easier to fill the barrels, then she secured her under the trees and unhitched the harness.

"There you go girl, water to drink and lots of grass for grazin'. Your work's done for now, but I gotta get busy." Laura patted the horse's neck, then turned back to the wagon.

"Best get started. No sense standing here staring at the water with these empty barrels to fill." She lifted her skirt hem and secured the material to her waistband, not wanting it to drag in the water while she worked.

Grabbing the metal bucket, she walked into the river to fill it, then carried it back to the wagon. The heavy bucketful barely covered the bottom of the barrel. She sighed, then returned to the river to fill the bucket again and again.

By the time three of the barrels were full, Laura's muscles trembled with exhaustion. "Got to cool off

'fore I keel over," she said, wiping the sweat that dripped from her face.

She glanced at Star, resting in shade between two tall trees as she grazed, switching her tail now and then. The gentle horse was the only living thing in sight near the slow flowing river. The sun was just past the zenith, beginning its western track to the horizon. No wonder there are no birds or critters around, too hot for 'em out here. Too bad the bugs don't mind the heat cause it'd sure be nice if they were all hidin' out, too.

Pulling her skirt up higher, well above her knees, Laura secured it with care, then marched into the river until the cool water covered her lower legs. "Oh," she groaned as the water chilled her skin, the slow current tugging as it flowed around her thighs. "That feels so good."

Laura leaned over, cupping water in both hands, then rubbed it over the parched skin on her face, arms, and chest. The tips of her braids fell into the water, but she didn't care. Refreshed and energized, Laura laughed and stepped out of the cool current, feeling rivulets running down the back of her dress from the wet braids. She untucked her skirt and walked to the front of the wagon. She reached for her dinner pail. Time to eat.

There was only one empty barrel left when Pa came galloping up toward the wagon. What was Pa doing here? Something must be bad wrong. Was one of the girls hurt?

Laura stepped out of the water and watched Pa throw the reins down, ground-tying the lathered horse where it stood. He grabbed Laura's arm and jerked her around to face him.

"I know what you did," he said, spittle flying from his mouth. "Not bad enough acting the harlot like your whore of a sister, but exposing yourself to your brother?"

"I never . . ." Laura's mouth opened in shock at his words.

"Don't lie to me," Pa yelled, face red with fury. "Ben tol' me that when he came to help you with the water, you were in the river with your dress up, legs bare right up to your bloomers. Leanin' way over, showin' your chest, teasin', smilin', and wavin' right at him the whole time."

Laura couldn't believe what she was hearing. The words were so ugly, the foul images spilling like poison from Pa's mouth. She shook her head, unable to breathe, stunned by the terrible accusation.

"You're lucky Ben's just a boy. Actin' like a bitch in heat around a man will get you jumped like a dog." Pa's anger only increased in response to Laura's denial. "No, no, I never." Laura continued to shake her head. She stepped back just as Pa slapped her face. The force of his blow knocked her down and set her face on fire.

Then Pa dropped on top of Laura, his legs pinned her to the ground and one forearm shoved tight against her throat. "Just like your ma. She was always sashayin' around, had men sniffin' after her like dogs ever'where she went. Lied about it too. Didn't know her place."

Laura tried to fight her way free, terrified and desperate to breathe, gasping and coughing, but unable to push Pa's arm away from her neck.

"Your ma fought me too, at first," Pa said, his eyes glazed. "Till I broke her. Guess I haf'ta break you, too."

Pa shoved Laura's dress up w

With one hand, then jerked her bloomers down, ripping the fabric away from her body. Pa forced her legs apart as he held her down, his body crushing her. Then he reached back and fumbled with his pants, both knees trapping her in place. "No man can let a woman disobey him. You better learn that right now."

Laura's terror was suddenly eclipsed by pain, absolute agony that felt like she was being ripped apart. She couldn't move with her pa's weight holding her down, his body slamming into her over and over. Finally, Pa collapsed on top of her, his breathing loud, rasping, his body pouring sweat. Laura kept her eyes closed as tight as she could, a futile attempt to block out what was happening, but she was unable to escape the sound of Pa's breathing and the foul smell of his hot breath on her face and neck.

His wet skin felt slimy and wrong everywhere it touched her.

After what seemed an eternity, Pa stood up, adjusting his clothes. "Actin' the whore gets you treated like a whore. Can't blame nobody but yourself."

Laura lay still, pain wracking every part of her body. She was afraid to move and unwilling to open her eyes and face Pa looming above her.

"Go clean yourself up, then finish fillin' those barrels." Laura heard Pa move away, then mount his horse. "Don't even think about talkin' about this unless you want the strap. And I better never hear about you showin' yourself off to Ben again."

The sounds of Pa's galloping horse faded away, but Laura still didn't move or open her eyes. Her mind was numb, but the soothing sound of the river and the buzzing of insects began to intrude. The stinging bites of flies settling on her bloody legs finally forced her to move. Each tiny movement was slow and painful. First, she rose to her knees, entire body shaking, then to her feet. Sweat, rank from heat and fear, glued clothing to her wet skin. Blood ran down her trembling legs, thick on both inner thighs. She removed her torn bloomers from around her ankles and tossed them aside.

Laura hobbled to the water, every step a major effort against the throbbing pain that engulfed her entire body. She walked into the current until it rippled around her thighs, almost to her waist. When she sat down, the material of her dress ballooned away from her body, as if trying to escape.

Laura dipped her hands into the water and started scouring her face and arms. Her lips were bleeding from where she'd bitten them. The scratches where Pa had clawed into her arms stung and burned. Her battered face now ached from the intense scrubbing. Next she tried to clean the blood from her legs and lower body. Laura kept washing herself long after the dirt and gore were gone, unable to stop, stained clear through her body and soul.

Laura leaned forward, arms clasped around her body, as the cold water swirled around her. How could Pa do such a thing to her?

She wished she could let go and float down the river forever, never looking back. Maybe go all the way to the ocean, or just drown and wash up on the bank like the raccoon they'd found last week. Anything would be better than goin' home. Anythin', anythin' at all, would be better than goin' home.

With great reluctance Laura got back on her feet, ignoring the cold, wet dress plastered to her body. She forced herself to finish filling the last barrel, then secured the barrel lids. Every single step, every movement hurt, but somehow, she managed to hitch Star back to the wagon, then pulled herself up on the bench, and started toward home.

The trip seemed to take forever but wasn't nearly long enough. She went straight to the barn, grateful that only Daisy was there. The mule reached out and tried to nuzzle for some attention but Laura pushed the soft, whiskery muzzle away. She simply didn't have enough energy to respond with more.

She put the wagon and horse away. It was too late to empty the barrels, but that could be done in the morning. She hated leaving the barn to go inside the house, but there was no place else to go.

When she walked through the door, Lizbeth was at the stove stirring something in a big pot, while Becca stood at the counter slicing bread. Bonnie was pulling the table away from the wall. "Supper's almost ready," Lizbeth glanced up and said. "Help Bonnie get the table ready."

Laura nodded, unable to speak, and walked to the table to help her sister. The rich smell of stew filled the room and everything looked ordinary, but she felt anything but normal.

"You look awful peaked," Becca said, staring at Laura. "Are you sick from the heat? Kinda surprisin' since the river is nice and cool. And your face is all swelled up."

"I fell and banged my cheek on the side of the wagon. I'm alright. Just tired out." Laura's response was curt, but she didn't care. Talking made it too easy for the tears to start, and she couldn't risk answering any questions.

Pa and Ben came inside as the girls were putting food on the table. Pa never looked at Laura or said a word to her. His silence didn't matter though since she felt sick inside just because he was in the room. Ben didn't say anything either but smirked at her when no one could see.

Once supper was cleared away and the evening chores completed, Laura was the first to lie down on her pallet. She curled into a tight ball and hid behind closed eyelids, pretending to be asleep. She kept her breathing even as she listened to everyone else settle down for the night. What seemed like hours of sheer torture passed as visions of what happened earlier kept replaying in her head.

After everyone else fell asleep and the sound of Pa's snoring filled the room, an old, forgotten memory popped into Laura's mind like an ugly nightmare. Pa's voice came from behind the blanket, but she couldn't understand his words. The sudden sound of hard slaps came after, each followed by a low cry of pain. Seconds later came the rhythmic creaking of the rope mattress, accompanied by guttural grunting she now recognized as coming from Pa.

Oh no, Ma went through what he did to me, too. How could she stand to lie next to him every night, never knowing when he'd attack her again? Laura's skin crawled just being in the house with Pa now. How could Ma have endured it?

The two images flowed together in Laura's mind, the old memory she now understood, and the ghastly recollection of what Pa did to her that day. Nausea overwhelmed Laura, propelling her out the door. Her icy hands pressed against her lips to hold back the flood that threatened to spew from her mouth. She headed for the privy, running as fast as she could while inhaling deep breaths of the cool night air through her nose.

Laura didn't quite make it, heaving over and over into the weeds a few yards short of the outhouse door. She clasped her arms around her body as she bent over until the retching passed, long after her stomach was empty. Laura straightened up, wiped her mouth with the back of her hand, and then heard something move in the weeds behind her. She froze in place, afraid to turn around.

"Guess you won't be disrespectin' me anymore, after Pa got through with you," Ben whispered. "I tol' you you'd be sorry for talkin' to me the way you did." Laura turned around to see her brother right behind her. "You lied to Pa. I never did what you said. You lied."

"No, I didn't." Ben laughed. "You did ever' single thing I said you did. Just 'cause you didn't know I was watchin' don't mean I lied." He snickered. "Not my fault Pa took it the way he did." Ben reached out, touching Laura's chest just above the top of her nightgown, then grabbed the fabric and started to pull it down, trailing the back of his hand against her skin. Laura jerked the cloth away from Ben's hands and jumped back away from him. She ran inside the privy, locked herself in, and leaned against the rough wood.

Seconds after the door was secured, she heard Ben's breathing on the other side.

"You can't stay in there forever. I'll be waitin' in the house for you. Things are goin' to be different from now on." Ben whistled as he strolled away.

CHAPTER FOURTEEN

Not Alone

With Ben's voice fading in her ears, Laura sank to her knees and leaned against the unfinished wooden door for support, terrified by his parting words. The tiny space was dark, with only the moonlight that filtered through the crescent-shaped cut-out near the top of the door and the circular holes on both side walls. The air stank from the contents of the pit since the vents were located just below the sloped roof and did little to filter the foul air.

Laura was afraid if she started crying again, she'd never be able to stop. Her body shook so hard it was difficult to breathe, but there were no more tears.

What could she do? After what Pa did, she'd never be safe again. And Ben? He's worse'n Pa, 'cause he loves to hurt people just for the fun of it. No tellin' what he might say to Pa next time, or what he'd do to her himself.

All at once Laura took a deep breath, her body rigid and steady. Anger replaced her fear. "No, no, I ain't takin' it anymore," she said out loud. "Ruth got away, and I can too. They're not gonna touch me again."

Laura unhooked the latch, taking great care to avoid making any noise, pushed the door open and stepped outside. She shut the door behind her to close the nasty smell inside and filled her lungs with the still night air.

The house was just a deep shadow against the darkness of the night. Laura stood motionless for a long time until she was sure Ben was no longer lurking outside. She decided she was never goin' in that house again, don't matter if she was barefoot and just wearin' a nightgown. Laura looked up at the night sky with clouds floating in front of the stars and the narrow sliver of moon. She took another deep breath, then turned away from the house and began to walk down the familiar path.

Ruth'd help, she just had to get to her. Laura'd gone down the road hundreds of times. It was no different just cause it was dark.

Laura started toward the road, needing very little light to show the way. But the path, so easy to follow during the day, was not the same on that night. Tall grasses that rustled on both sides were changed by the darkness into images of Ben sneaking up on her, ready to pounce. Disturbed by Laura's unexpected passage, the noises made by startled birds taking flight became Ben's cruel laughter in her ear. Each familiar sound was transformed and terrifying, causing Laura's heart to race as she whirled around to check the darkness. She convinced herself that Pa and Ben were both after her and ran as fast as she could in the darkness until she tripped and fell.

Blind panic took over, causing Laura to repeat the same pattern of running and falling again and again. She lost track of how many times she went down, always landing on her hands and knees. Every time she picked herself back up and started again, there were more cuts and scratches on her hands and legs that burned and bled.

But Laura couldn't stop, no matter how scared she was. Wouldn't even matter if somethin' jumped out and got her. That'd still be better than goin' back. Just had to keep on till she got to Ruth.

"Stop!" a woman's voice shouted in Laura's mind. "Get off the road right now."

The urgency of the command compelled Laura to leap into the tall weeds at the side of the path.

"Farther. You mustn't be seen from the road."

Without a thought, Laura obeyed and burrowed in deeper and deeper, fear pushing her on until she was sure no one could see her from the road.

"Stay still and don't make a sound," the voice ordered. The faint sounds of a horse and buggy on the road reached Laura's ears. "Sound carries a long way at night. Don't move a muscle." Hunkered down, surrounded by tall whispering stems, Laura obeyed.

Wait a minute. Who was she hiding from? Laura rose up to her knees.

"I know you're tired, Belle, me too. Not

much longer and we'll be home. Wouldn't be nearly so late iffen that baby hadn't been turned the wrong way."

That was Miz Dobbs comin' down the road. She'd help me. Laura started to stand, taking a deep breath to call for help.

"No, stay down." the voice insisted. "Miz Dobbs can't keep you away from your pa, 'cause you're still a child. Don't make a sound."

Startled, Laura obeyed, listening to Miz Dobbs pass by on the road. The voice in her mind hummed a sweet, familiar tune that helped her stay still.

Then Laura couldn't hear the wagon anymore. She stood up, muscles stiff and protesting every move. The voice was gone. She waited a moment for it to return but heard only insects and night birds. Making as little noise as possible, she worked her way back to the path. Could Ben be waiting for her on the road?

Laura's mind filled with scary images as she faced the final steps out into the open, but the soft humming started again, calming her fears.

"I can do this," Laura whispered to

herself. "I got to get to Ruth." She took a deep breath, then stepped out of hiding, making sure the path was empty before resuming her trek.

By the time she saw the faint outlines of the buildings in town, Laura's body was beyond exhaustion. The dim light of the crescent moon was aided by a rose whisper of dawn on the horizon, just a tiny softening of the darkness to help her see her way.

She stepped up on the wooden sidewalk and walked to the Carpenter's store. She went into a narrow alley between it and the neighboring building and turned left at the back. Then she felt her way toward a flight of stairs up to the second floor where Paul's family lived. Ruth's room had been used for storing inventory, but it didn't have a separate entrance. She needed to find Ruth and wake her up without disturbing Paul's family.

Luck was with her. Laura found Ruth's window unlocked and opened just an inch to let in the night air. "Ruth," she whispered, bent down so her mouth was next to the narrow opening at the base of the window. "Ruth, I need you."

The rhythm of Ruth's breathing didn't

change, so Laura inserted her fingers and pressed them up against the bottom of the window. She lifted it all the way up, trying hard not to make a sound. The window was small, a very tight fit, but Laura's sheer determination helped her push her body through the opening, where she dropped on the floor with a soft thump.

She went to the bed and leaned down next to her sister's ear. "Ruth, Ruth, please wake up. I need you," she whispered.

"What?" Ruth startled awake and sat up. "What happened? How'd you get in here? Have you been walking all night?"

Laura burst into tears, no longer able to hold them back.

"You're safe now, I promise nobody'll hurt you here." Ruth held Laura in her arms, rocking and soothing her until the tears slowed. "Tell me what happened."

"Pa raped me. I can't go back there. I'm afraid of Ben too. Pa did it cause Ben told him some filthy lies about me, just like he did about you before."

"Oh, no," Ruth cried. She held Laura in her arms. "I've got to get help. You mustn't go back, but we can't let Pa find you or you'll have no choice. I know it's hard, but you need to tell me exactly what happened."

By the time Laura finished her story, they were both crying. Ruth jumped up and lit the lantern that rested on a small table near the bed. "Don't worry. I'll be right back." She hurried out of the room.

Laura sat on Ruth's bed while she waited for her sister to return, terrified and embarrassed about having to ask strangers for help. Would they believe her? What if Pa came? She couldn't go back to him. She'd rather die. With her arms wrapped tightly around herself, she rocked back and forth as she waited for what seemed like hours.

"It's gonna be alright," Ruth said when she came back into the room. She knelt down in front of Laura and lifted her chin up. "Paul's family will help. Come on into the front room so we can plan what to do." She helped Laura to her feet. "Don't worry, we'll take care of you."

Ruth wrapped her arm around Laura's waist and led her into the next room. Laura stopped moving and pulled back when she saw the grim looks on Paul's parents' faces.

"Honey, don't you worry," Miz

Carpenter said, seeing the fear on Laura's face. "We're just tryin' to figure out what to do."

"We believe you," Paul said, reaching out to both sisters, wrapping his arms around them. "Ruth will always have scars on her back from what your pa did to her, so we know what he's capable of. There's no way we'll let him hurt you, again, Laura."

"Got to get you away fast," Mr. Carpenter said. "Soon as he wakes up, your pa will figure you've run to Ruth for help and come here. If he goes straight to the Sheriff for help first, they'll force you to go back. We've got to think of a safe place for you to go where your Pa can't find you."

"Emma!" Miz Carpenter whirled around to face her husband. "Jake, I'm sure Emma would take Laura in and nobody in town knows her or where she lives."

Emma? Who was this Emma that nobody knew? What if she didn't believe Laura? What if she sent her back to Pa?

"She'd be perfect," Mr. Carpenter said. "I'll get the wagon and bring it out back. Martha, you'll have to take Laura by yourself, and she'll need to hide under blankets until you get out of town. We can't risk somebody seeing her with you and telling the Sheriff. Stay at Emma's place for the night so nobody can figure out how far you went, then come back the next day."

Laura was surprised to see Mr. Carpenter give his wife a hug and kiss her on the forehead before he continued speaking. "I don't like sending you so far alone, but I need to be here to face Cavanaugh and the Sheriff tomorrow. Wouldn't be right to leave Paul and Ruth to handle it by themselves."

Mr. Carpenter watched his wife head to their room to get ready for the trip, then leaned down to look into Laura's face. "My wife's sister, Emma, is a very good woman. She's always taking in stray animals and people, whenever she thinks they need help. We'll get you out of here, but you'll have to do exactly as I say. I know you hate to leave your sister, but it's not safe for you here."

"Are you sure? Takin' in a stranger is askin' a lot," Laura said. "I don't want to get you all in trouble."

Miz Carpenter, fully dressed and ready to go, returned, then bent down and gave Laura a quick, reassuring hug. "He's right. And you can't leave bare-foot in a nightgown," she said.

"I'm going down to the store to get some clothes, shoes, and personal supplies for you. Ruth, I'll need your help to get what she'll need, and we've got to hurry. While we're doing that, Laura, you need to use the washbasin and clean all those cuts and scratches."

"Yes ma'am," Laura said and went to Ruth's room to wash. Looking in the mirror, an expression of sheer terror stared back. All strangers? She was goin' to be with nothing but strangers? What if they didn't like her? What if they didn't believe her? Will they really protect her from Pa?

Within a short time, a clean, neat Laura, dressed in new clothes, was hidden by stacks of blankets, clothing, and household items in the wagon bed. Miz Carpenter drove away under the watchful eyes of her family. If the wagon was stopped, she'd say that the things in the wagon were for her sister's family. It would be a long trip, but she had a loaded shotgun tucked by her feet for protection.

Laura planned on joining Miz Carpenter on the driver's bench as soon as they were out of town, but she was lulled into an exhausted sleep by the motion of the wagon. She slept for several hours until the wagon stopped. She was afraid to move until she heard Miz Carpenter's voice.

"Come on out now, it's safe." Miz Carpenter shook Laura's shoulder, after moving the blankets away from her. "Climb down and stretch your legs."

"Where are we?" Laura looked around.

"Just a couple of hours from Emma's place." Miz Carpenter had driven the wagon about a half-mile off the road and stopped near a tiny, narrow stream that twisted between a double line of willow trees. She unhitched the horse, then led him to the water to drink. "Sargent needs a break, and we can use one, too." When the horse finished drinking, she tied him to a tree near the wagon so he could graze and carried a picnic basket into a small patch of shade.

"Come sit with me, Laura," she said, patting the ground next to her. "I need to tell you about Emma, so you'll know what to expect. And you've got to be hungry, so we'll eat while we talk."

Laura hadn't thought about food, but the sight and smell of the thick fried-egg and bacon sandwich Miz Carpenter handed her made her mouth water. "Is Miss Emma your older sister?" Laura asked, after taking a bite.

"No, she was the baby. There were four of us girls although Amy passed away many years ago. Emma was always pretty as a picture, but strong-willed and stubborn. She was smart as a whip too and scared all the young men away. She taught school for years. Never did get married. When Pa died from a snake bite, she quit teaching and took over running the farm for Ma."

A big smile lit up Miz Carpenter's face. "More than one man told Ma she'd have to sell since Pa wasn't around to take care of things, but Emma proved 'em all wrong. Then, when Ma passed on, Emma got the farm and has taken care of everything all by herself. Ma always said Emma could do anything she set her mind to."

Laura listened with rapt attention, understanding how important it was to remember what she was being told.

"Two things Emma can't abide," Miz Carpenter said, looking into Laura's eyes. "Don't ever lie to her and never let her think you're lazy. She's got a good heart but has no patience for lies or laziness."

"I don't lie, Miz Carpenter," Laura insisted. "But will Miss Emma believe me? Pa and Ben are always calling me a liar. They never believe me and say awful things."

"I believe you, and Emma will too. She knows the truth when she hears it," Miz Carpenter said. "And why don't you call me Miz Martha from now on, since we'll be family when Paul and Ruth get married. Come on, we need to get back on the road," Miz Martha said, rising to her feet. "The sooner we mke it to Emma's place, the sooner you can settle in."

They rode in silence, sitting side by side on the wagon bench, for the next hour. Miz Martha asked a few questions, but Laura responded with one-word answers. After awhile Miz Martha reached out and touched Laura's hand. "Something's bothering you, why don't you tell me what it is?"

Laura hesitated, took a deep breath and then said, "Long's I can remember, Pa's been tellin' Ruth and me that we take after Ma. He said she was no good, didn't know her place, and was always whorin' around." Laura kept her eyes down as she spoke, clenching her fists in her lap so hard the knuckles were white. "He kept sayin' it over and over when he beat

Ruth, and then again when he was on top a me. He said what he did was all our fault,' cause of the way we acted."

"Stop right there," Miz Martha said. "I knew your ma, and she was a good woman. She was quiet as can be, never even looked people in the face. She was a very pretty woman though, so maybe your pa just didn't like thinking that other men would look at her. Your ma couldn't help that. She didn't do anything wrong, and neither did you nor Ruth. I don't like speaking bad about somebody's kin, but your pa is a cruel, mean man."

Miz Martha reached out and touched Laura's hand. She said "Not one word your Pa said about your ma, about Ruth, or about you, was true. And no man has the right to do what he did to either of you. You need to put his words right outta your head, you hear me?" Laura nodded, afraid that she might start crying, but so relieved and grateful.

By the time Emma's place came into view, Laura couldn't keep her eyes open. But when the two story white house with pretty blue trim came into sight, her exhaustion disappeared.

"Is that it? I've never been in a house that big."

"Pa built it for Ma when they got married. He promised her he'd build a house they could fill with young'uns and not feel crowded," Miz Martha said. "Though we felt pretty crowded with us four girls and lots of our friends running in and out all the time. Ma loved having people around, and Pa loved whatever made Ma happy."

Wondering about the figure standing on the porch wearing trousers, Laura asked, "Who does Miss Emma live with?"

Miz Martha laughed and said, "That's Emma, and she lives alone except for the help. Never has worried much about what folks think."

Sure enough, when the wagon got closer to the house, Laura saw that trousers and a man's shirt could not hide a distinctly feminine figure topped by dark hair pulled up in a messy bun above a strong-featured face.

"Martha, my word," Emma shouted, then jumped off the porch, running toward them.

Miz Martha leaped from the wagon bench, straight into a bear hug with her sister.

Laura watched, wide-eyed, never having seen grown-ups jumping up and down, hugging like little ones.

"Emma, this is Laura," Martha said. "Her sister Ruth's gonna marry Paul soon, so she'll be family."

"Glad to meet you, Laura," Emma said with a smile. "I'm guessing you need some help for Martha to bring you here, so let's all go inside. I'll fix us something to eat while you tell me what's going on. Don't worry, I'll have a couple of the hands unload everything, and take care of the horse and wagon."

Laura followed Martha and Emma into the house. She looked around from one amazing sight to another. She never imagined a ceilin' that high up. How could anybody ever reach to sweep the cobwebs? Laura's head kept turning from one wonder to another. Who would a thought floors could be as shiny as the furniture? And she noticed other pretty things everywhere, on the tables and even the walls. Then Laura's eyes met Miss Emma's, and she dreaded the thought of having to tell her horrible story. It seemed wrong to bring such ugliness into a house full of beautiful things.

Emma didn't look like any woman Laura

had ever seen. Her back was straight as a soldier's. Her hands were large but well-shaped, and the clothing she wore somehow managed to look feminine and attractive even though they were designed for men. "Martha, why don't you show Laura Dorothy's old room. I think she'd be comfortable there, don't you?" Emma smiled at Laura as if she could read her thoughts. "I'll start fixing something for us to eat."

"Good idea," Martha said, motioning Laura toward the staircase. "I'll carry that satchel up for you. Just follow me. Your room will be two doors to the right at the top of the stairs."

Laura followed Martha to the room's open doorway, then looked around in amazement. "Never seen a room like this before," she said, staring at the bright colored patchwork quilt that covered the bed, the white painted furniture, and butter yellow curtains that billowed around the window. Laura found it hard to breath, afraid to touch anything in such a magical space.

"Ma let each of us girls decorate our rooms however we wanted. She thought if we made them pretty, we'd take pride in keeping them clean and neat. Ma's idea never worked for Dorothy, though. Her room didn't look this nice when she lived at home, and she still can't keep a tidy house," Martha said with a smile as she dropped Laura's bag on the seat of a white rocker in front of the window. "Come on now, let's go help Emma with the table."

Laura was grateful that neither Martha nor Emma wanted to talk while they were eating. The food, crispy salt-pork, potatoes, green beans cooked in the drippings, and fresh bread with butter, was delicious washed down with cool milk. As her stomach filled, Laura's eyes drifted closed, and she fought to stay awake.

"Honey," Emma said, touching Laura's hand, "Why don't you go to your room, wash up and head to bed? Martha and I have lots of catching up to do, but you need to sleep. Don't worry, we'll have all the time we need to talk tomorrow when you're rested and ready."

"Yes, ma'am," Laura said, so sleepy she found it difficult to form her words. "Thank you so much."

Grateful to escape from having to tell her story again, she went to the stairs and began to climb. She hung on the banister to pull leaden feet up each step. When Laura reached the beautiful bedroom, she washed her face in the washbasin on the dresser. Then she looked through the satchel Miz Martha had placed on the rocking chair, found a soft pink nightgown and put it on. Laura pulled the quilt back and climbed in the bed, placed her head in the middle of the pillow and tugged the quilt up to her shoulders.

She'd never slept on a real bed before. Sure was a lot softer than a pallet on the floor. Kind of felt like floating. She curled on her side, her face cooled by the pillow's soft cotton cover. And a real pillow 'stead of a rolled piece of quilt. She'd never felt anythin' so soft. The pillow felt like it was full a feathers.

Laura didn't drop off to sleep right away because she couldn't help feeling something was wrong. She soon realized that, for the first time in her life, she was sleeping in a room all alone without the soothing sounds of her sisters around her.

I hope they're alright. Poor Bonnie's gonna have a hard time without me. Who's gonna take her to school? She'll be too scared to walk alone. All of a sudden, Laura was overwhelmed with guilt for leaving her little sister behind. She whispered "I had to get away. Nothin' else I could do. I'm sorry Bonnie.

CHAPTER FIFTEEN

New Life

Laura woke in stages, feeling warm and comfortable curled up in bed. She opened her eyes. Disoriented at first by the strange surroundings, she sat up, blinked and rubbed the sleep from her eyes. Then scenes from the day before flashed through her mind—the sound of Ben's menacing voice, the stink of the dark outhouse, the long walk through the night to Ruth, the trip to Miss Emma's house.

She leaped out of bed and ran to the window. The sun was shining hot and bright high in the sky, A woman in the yard was swinging a long-handled wooden rug-beater against a carpet draped over a rope strung between two posts. Laura saw a puff of dust fly each time the round, patterned head hit the heavy fabric. In the distance, another woman hoed a row of potatoes in a garden area. Even farther away, three men on horseback were following a herd of slow-moving cattle.

Laura realized that the sun was at its zenith and everybody was out working. She had slept through the whole morning. Miz Martha had told Laura that Miss Emma couldn't abide laziness, and there she was, sleeping half the day away. Laura washed and dressed as fast as she could. She started toward the door, then turned back to make the bed and put her nightgown into one of the drawers. When she was sure the room looked as neat as when she found it, Laura sprinted out of the room and down the stairs, her heart racing with fear and shame.

Miss Emma was sitting alone in the dining room, sorting through some papers, her reading glasses perched on the end of her nose, when Laura entered the room. Emma was wearing a pair of men's trousers and a man's long-sleeved blue shirt with the sleeves rolled up almost to her elbows and wore her hair twisted into a neat coil at the nape of her neck. Laura swallowed hard and tried to get her breathing under control.

"Miss Emma, I'm so sorry. I know better

than to sleep late like this. I don't know how it happened, but I promise it won't happen again."

"I know." Miss Emma pushed the papers aside and rested her forearms on the table. She removed her glasses and leaned forward, a fierce look on her face as she met Laura's eyes.

"Martha and I both thought you needed to rest and heal. She told me what happened yesterday, and about what your pa did to Ruth. We talked everything out before Martha left and agreed on what to do. But it won't be easy."

Laura took a deep breath, determined to be strong, and returned Miss Emma's gaze with an intense look of her own. Hands clenched in her lap and shoulders hunched forward, Laura felt like her whole body was tight as a bow string. "Whatever you want me to do, Miss Emma. I ain't scared of hard work, and I'm a fast learner. If you can let me stay, I'll do whatever you ask." Laura dropped her eyes and bent forward, rubbing her hands up and down her arms. "I'm not afraid of much, but I'm real scared of Pa and Ben. I can't go back there, Miss Emma, I just can't," Laura said, unable to control the shaking in her voice.

"Don't you worry about that. I agree with Martha that we have to keep you safe from them." Miss Emma leaned forward, the fingers of each hand touching above the table, pointed at Laura. "What I'd really like to do is take a shotgun to both of 'em like I do to vermin here on the farm, but don't think I could get away with that." Miss Emma smirked, then continued. "Since that idea's out the window, let's see about getting something for you to eat."

She stood up and led Laura out of the dining room to the outside kitchen, her stride purposeful with no wasted motions. When they reached the fragrant kitchen, she introduced Laura to a small, older woman kneading bread dough on a long table covered with flour and several loaves rising in cloth-covered bowls. Her big chocolate colored eyes met Laura's. She'd pulled her gray hair back into a tight bun that framed a round, tanned face covered with fine wrinkles, like parchment, bisected by a huge smile. The woman's short, squat body showed her age, but every movement with the dough revealed corded muscles in her strong forearms and hands.

"Miz Mary this is Laura. Laura this is Miz Mary, no doubt the best darn cook in the state." Miz Mary and Laura smiled at one another, then Miss Emma continued. "Laura's going to stay with us. Can you fix some food for her? She was so tuckered out from traveling yesterday that she slept right through breakfast. Just put a plate on the table, so she can eat after I show her around."

"Yes, ma'am," Miz Mary said with a grin and a wink at Laura. "As soon as I set this dough to risin', I'll get right to it."

"Thanks, Mary," Emma said. "Come on, Laura, I'll show you the house, and we can talk about what chores you'll be doing."

Laura followed Miss Emma back inside, then upstairs where they looked into each of the four bedrooms. All were the same size and layout, opening off the hallway at the top of the stairs. The rooms were square, about ten feet on each side, with one large curtained window right across from the door. They all had a bed, a bureau with three drawers set underneath a framed mirror, and a rocking chair. A washbasin sat in each room on top of the chest of drawers. A multi-colored, circular hooked rug laid in the center of the polished wooden floor. The furniture was arranged the same in each room, but the color schemes of the curtains and bedding were all different, soft blue, deep green, warm brown, and the yellow in Laura's room. Only Laura's was occupied, but the other three were neat and clean, beds made up ready for guests.

Emma led the way back to the staircase. "All our hired hands stay out in the bunkhouses, one for women and one for men. You're too young to be out there and family as well, so you'll stay up here."

"Yes, ma'am." Laura bobbed her head, paying close attention to every word.

"Besides, we don't want any of the hands asking too many questions. We're a long way from your pa, but you never know how idle talk gets spread. Hired hands come and go all the time, spreading gossip each new place they go. Nobody needs to know how old you are, where you're from, or why you're here. I'll pass word out that you're kin. That'll keep 'em quiet."

Miss Emma turned and looked straight at Laura. "I'm not asking you to lie or be rude, but you can't be talking about your family or where you come from. And nothing ever about what your pa did. Understand? Best be polite, but not get too friendly with anyone."

"Yes, Miss Emma, I'll be careful. Too hard to talk about, anyways." Laura's gaze dropped down, and she stared at the floor. "Not used to talkin' to strangers, wouldn't know how to. Sure won't answer no questions from folks I don't know."

"Good. Now, since you'll be stayin' up here, it'll be up to you to keep all the bedrooms clean. Sweeping and dusting every other day. When guests come, you'll have to make sure the washbasins have fresh water each day, then empty and clean the chamberpots in the morning. Don't have guests too often, but when they're here, we treat 'em right. Dorothy got away with being a mess, but I can't abide it. Make your bed and straighten the room before coming to breakfast, so all the bedrooms look just right and we'll get along fine."

That said, Miss Emma led Laura into the dining room and took her place at the table. "Go ahead, sit yourself down and eat," she said, pointing to the plate across the table from her chair.

Laura sat down and stared at a stack of

steaming griddlecakes, smothered in butter and syrup, with a tall cool glass of milk to wash them down. She picked up her fork, then cut a small golden square and raised it to her mouth.

After swallowing the first, sweet bite, she said, "Don't think I've ever tasted anythin' this good, not even in town."

"You can thank Miz Mary, I told you she's the best cook around."

"I surely will." Laura found it hard to believe folks ate like that all the time, and she would be stayin' in this grand house, with a room of her own. Didn't matter what chores Miss Emma gave her, couldn't be as hard as workin' at home.

Miss Emma sighed, then said, "When Martha and I talked about your pa, she told me about your ma, too, and what's been going on since she passed. Martha and Jake both love Ruth like a daughter already. They're happy as can be that she's marrying Paul, and that means they want to do right by you, too. Problem is, people don't like to see somebody messing in another family's business, especially not between a pa and his child. If your pa finds out you're here, there'll be nothing we can do to stop him from taking you back." An icy chill crept up Laura's spine and tightened around her chest. Her hands started to tremble. She dropped the fork onto the plate with a clatter, her appetite all of a sudden gone.

"Don't worry," Emma reached across the table and patted Laura's hand, "Martha and I talked a lot, and we think we can make sure that don't happen. Your pa's hopping mad right now, but in time he'll lose interest. Fact is, he'll probably start telling folks he sent you away just to save face.

The story we'll tell everyone is simple. I'll say that you're kin, a cousin twice removed. You're from Muskogee, but both your folks died when your house burned down, leaving you with no place to go. I've taken you in to live here now, and you'll work to earn your keep just like everybody else. Always better to tell the truth when you can, but we're changing it up a bit and leaving a lot out. Think you can do that?"

"Yes, ma'am," Laura took a deep breath. "I promise to work hard for you and not be a bother. Don' like talkin' about things anyways. Had a awful nightmare about what Pa done to me, but don' see how talkin' about it would help none."

"That's right. You got to just shut all that bad stuff away and not think about it. Talking won't change anything, so just leave all the bad in the past."

"I can do that, Miss Emma. Sure will miss my sisters though. I hate to think about them still with Pa, 'specially with him mad 'cause both Ruth and me got away."

"Can't help them, Laura. They'll have to deal with him the best way they can. You might write to Ruth every now and then to let her know you're alright, and she maybe could tell you about the others. You'll both have to be careful what goes on paper though, because sometimes letters get misdirected or opened by accident." Emma pursed her lips and shook her head. "Nobody should have to worry about the mail, but you never know about folks."

"I'll be real careful. I'm good with my letters, and with Ruth at the store, she'll know what's happenin'." Miss Emma stood up. "Good. Take your plate out to Miz Mary, then change into a pair of those trousers Miz Martha brought for you. When you're ready, meet me out at the barn. We'll ride the property, so you can see where things are, then we'll figure out what chores are best for you."

"Yes ma'am," Laura gathered up her dishes. She'd do whatever it took to stay with Miss Emma. Not ever was she goin' to let Pa, Ben, nor anybody else hurt her again.

CHAPTER SIXTEEN

Thirteen

As Laura rode with Emma around the farm, she was almost overwhelmed with awe as they rode past rich fields and sturdy buildings.

Emma's mount was a spirited, tall sorrel gelding with white socks, whose light brown coat flashed red highlights in the sun as he danced his way along. Laura rode a palomino mare with a gait like a rocking horse. Miss Emma watched Laura, measuring her expertise on horseback, while giving a running commentary about the farm as they rode through the different fields.

Laura turned to Emma, her voice filled with wonder as she said, "Compared to Pa's farm, this place is like a whole different world."

"Probably not so different, just bigger."Laura thought about the sod house she'd grown up in, with dirt floors and a muslin ceiling that prevented wiggling vermin from falling on her. Miss Emma's house, with its smooth, bright-colored paint and big rooms with all the windows and shiny wooden floors was nothing like her old place. Fact is, the outdoor kitchen could hold Pa's whole house. And even the outdoor kitchen had wood floors 'stead of dirt. And her ma's old garden wouldn't take up more than a tiny corner of Miss Emma's truck garden. Laura wished her ma and sisters could see the place. They'd near faint walkin' through the garden. And the house? They wouldn't believe it was real unless they saw it for themselves

"This place is so big," Laura said. "You must need a lot of help to do all the work. Can't see a family bein' able to do it by themselves."

"It is big, and yes, we've always had help working it. My Pa bought 300 acres to start, then built the house for Ma. Every chance he got, he'd buy more land." Miss Emma led the way to the shore of a shallow, swift-flowing creek with Laura close behind. The two horses dropped their heads and drank from the cool water. Only when the animals had slaked their thirst did Miss Emma resume the tour.

"Pa was lucky to have money when he

started out, so when neighbors couldn't keep going and wanted to sell out, they knew he'd pay a fair price," Miss Emma said. "He ended up with about 700 acres, and I bought another 100 after he passed on. Takes a lot of work, so I'm always watching for good hands. Some folks who work for me have been here for years while others seem to come and go all the time."

"Ma would've loved this place, but Pa would'a been almost sick jealous," Laura said. "If there was a farm like this anywheres near our town, he'd be bad-mouthin' the owners for somethin' just out'a spite. I think Ma'd be happy to see me here."

Chores at Miss Emma's house were much different than at Laura's, so she had to relearn almost everything. She was used to rolling up a pallet when she woke up and storing it under Pa's bed. Now she had to make up the bed each morning just the way Miss Emma taught her and change the linens every other week. Caring for a dirt floor by sprinkling it to keep the dust down before sweeping was a whole lot different than keeping Miss Emma's wood floors clean and shiny. She learned to hate the process of rubbing in linseed oil though whether it was for floors or wooden furniture.

Laura loved spending time in the kitchen which always smelled of warm dough and sweet spices. She couldn't seem to improve her cooking skills, however, no matter how hard she tried.

"Watch me," Miz Mary said over and over, as she demonstrated the proper way to work bread dough. "Every lady needs to know how to make bread for her family."

"Yes ma'am, I'm watchin'," Laura would say as she focused on every movement of Miz Mary's strong hands. She tried to mimic each step with her own handful of uncooperative dough. She watched and did her best, but her's never looked like Miz Mary's and never rose the same in the bowl. Laura guessed she'd spent too much time playin' with Bonnie and not enough time helpin' Ruth.

Laura couldn't seem to master canning vegetables either, and the food she cooked for Miss Emma never looked or tasted the same as Miz Mary's.

"Girl, you better hope your man isn't picky about his meals. Or maybe you can marry one that can afford to hire a cook for you," Miss Emma announced one day. From then on, Laura only did minor chores in the kitchen, such as putting pots and pans away, getting out spices and supplies as Miz Mary cooked, or helping prepare food, like chopping onions or shelling peas.

What Laura loved doing was working in the garden, and she was good at it. She liked chores where she could be more independent, instead of working within a group of hired hands. Her favorites involved the animals— caring for the chickens, feeding the pigs, goats, and cows, and anything involving the horses.

Miss Emma and Laura started each day with a hearty breakfast. The food was plentiful and delicious, and they'd talk about all kinds of things as they ate. Quite a contrast from a household where meals were silent affairs. Laura missed going to school, but sometimes she thought she learned more from Miss Emma than she ever had from Miz Gibson, her teacher at school.

After living with Miss Emma for a month, Laura had given up on being first to arrive for breakfast. Miss Emma always started her day at the dining-room table, surrounded by paperwork and newsprint.

"Good morning," Miss Emma said one morning as Laura pulled out her chair and sat down. Miss Emma's plate was piled high, steam wafting over the folded pages of the newspaper spread all around the breakfast dishes.

"Good morning." Laura settled herself in her place across from Miss Emma, and filled her plate from platters of eggs, grits, biscuits, slices of bacon, and fresh strawberries. Laura watched Miss Emma eat with one hand as she held the newspaper in the other. She waited until Miss Emma put the paper down next to her plate before asking, "What's in the paper today?"

"Nothing good. Tax protests holding up school projects, court news, all the usual articles complaining about crime. More stories about the war in Europe, too. Mark my words, we'll be joining in the fighting before too long."

"We might go to war?" Laura said, surprised.

Miss Emma pursed her lips. "Europe's been engulfed in fighting for two long years already. Don't tell me you haven't heard anything about what's happened already, such as the Battle of Jutland, the German offensive near Verdun, and the fighting that's going on now at the Somme River."

"No, ma'am. I'm sorry, but I don't know anything about them. Pa never talked about news or worldly things. After Ma passed, we didn't go to church anymore, and trips to town were just to buy supplies. Pa'd get mad if he found out we spent time talkin' to strangers."

Miss Emma snorted and shook her head. "That's just plain wrong. No excuse for such ignorance, and we're going to fix that starting today. You have to know what's going on in the world. It's not enough to just keep up with what's happening in your own town." Miss Emma gathered the newspaper pages together, put them back in order, then handed them to Laura. "I want you to read the papers when I'm done with them. Read every page, including the advertisements. You need to know the news, what things cost, and what the editorials are about. Pay close attention to what you read, and be ready to talk about what the stories mean. Don't think you can just repeat what the articles said, because I'll expect you to understand what they mean and how what's happening in the world affects us."

Laura took the newspapers in her hands, then placed them beside her on the table, excited about the prospect of studying them later.

"The world is changing so fast now, you need to keep up. One day, hope not too long in the future, women'll be voting right along with men and we'll need to be ready."

Laura had never heard such ideas, but nodded, eager to please Miss Emma. Pa would pitch a fit hearin' such talk. Laura could just hear him yellin' 'bout dumb women, and how men have to be in control. Wouldn't it be somethin' if Miss Emma was right about women voting?

"Enough about world news," Miss Emma said. "Today's your birthday, so you can choose what you'd like to do. Not every day you get to be thirteen."

"How did you know?" Laura tilted her head. "Martha told me. We always made birthdays special, so, no chores for you today. What would you like to do? I have to make some deliveries in town this morn-ing, so don't dilly dally around thinking about it."

Laura knew what she'd like to do but was

almost afraid to ask. Taking a deep breath, she said, "If I'm really, really, careful, could I play the piano in the music room?"

"Sure you can. If I'd known you were interested in playing, I would've let you before." Miss Emma stood and stepped away from the table. "I've got to go, but I'll be back before supper. Enjoy the piano long as you want."

Laura cleared the table, then rushed to the music room. She stepped inside the doorway and stood still, surveying every inch of the area with delicious anticipation. Several instruments were stored in the room—two guitars, a banjo, a violin, some harmonicas, an accordion. But Laura focused only on the upright piano. She walked to it, not quite believing she had permission to play.

The rosewood finish, polished to perfection, gleamed in the morning light. Even the cover that hid the keys was beautiful, with gold-colored hinges and a small gold-metal plate in the front, just below the curve, with the word Steinway in elegant script. Laura took a deep breath, then sat down on the needle-point cushion that topped the bench. She sat in silence for a few minutes, then reached out to touch the intricate carving on the sides of the instrument, and the two silky-smooth flat panels on the upright portion. She put her hands back in her lap, trying to work up the courage to take the next step. After one final deep breath, she reached out and lifted the cover from the keys.

Laura never, ever thought this could happen. She thought she could stay there forever.

Laura touched the keys with her index fingers, testing until she found the sounds she wanted, then played the alphabet song. Her confidence grew, and her speed increased until she could play the song all the way through without making any mistakes, singing along with the notes. She repeated the process with *London Bridge*, *Here We Go Round the Mulberry Bush*, *Amazing Grace*, *Silent Night*, and every tune she could remember.

Hours later, when Miss Emma came back to the house, she followed the sound of music, then stood in the doorway and watched Laura play with a look of utter bliss on her face.

"My goodness, girl," Miss Emma said,

strolling into the room until she stood next to the bench. "Have you been sitting here all day?"

"Didn't seem like a long time. And Miz Mary came and got me for dinner." Laura glanced up at Miss Emma, then back down to the keys, "Playin' this piano almost feels like I'm dreamin'."

"Well, let me help you a little. Pianos are meant to be played with all your fingers, not just one. And good piano players know how to read music and play anything rather than just picking out what they've heard."

Miss Emma leaned over Laura's shoulder and placed her hands on the keys. "You should always start with your fingers in the same place. See where my right thumb is? This key is called middle C. The two black keys are just to the right of it. Your right thumb should be on 'C', with the other fingers spread on the keys next to it." She lifted her fingers from the keyboard and sat down on the end of the bench. "Now you try."

"Like this?" Laura placed her hand where Miss Emma's had been.

"That's right. Now, your left hand also starts on 'C', but you put your little finger on the 'C' key to the left of middle 'C', with the other fingers on the next keys. The keys only go from 'A' through 'G', which is why each hand starts on 'C'. Go ahead, try it."

Immediately Laura's fingers found their proper positions on the keyboard. "What about the two keys in the middle with no fingers on 'em?"

"Your fingers are just where they're supposed to be. Don't worry about those keys in the middle, you'll play them by moving your thumbs over, because the thumbs play two keys each."

"What about the black keys?" Laura looked up and saw a huge grin on Miss Emma's face.

"They're called sharps and flats. If you play the white keys one after another, you can hear that they go up a full note, but the black keys are half-way between the white ones on either side. I know that sounds complicated, but if you try it, you'll hear what I mean."

Laura began to press first one white key after another, starting with her left hand, then on with the right, remembering to strike two notes with each thumb. Then she did it again but played both white and black keys. "I can hear what you mean," she said, excitement and awe in her voice.

"And you just played your first scales. Good piano players memorize where their fingers go and know what the notes should sound like. That way, you can learn lots of songs without having to watch the keys, just listen and you'll know where your fingers are, and which fingers you need to play the next notes."

"So that's how Miz Gibson did it," Laura said. "Our school teacher played without lookin', and I always wondered how her fingers knew where to go."

"That's how, by listening and practicing." Miss Emma stood up, stretched, and stepped behind the bench. "Stand up a minute, so I can get a music book out of the bench."

Laura's eyes widened as she watched Miss Emma lift the piano bench lid and select a paper book from a messy pile nestled inside the bench.

"This is the music book I learned from as a little girl. It's a mite tattered after all these years but should work just fine for you." Miss Emma opened the book and placed it in a narrow channel above the keys. Then she showed Laura how the scales and notes in the book corresponded to the keys she'd just played. "I'm going to change and check on Miz Mary in the kitchen. You go ahead and play all you want. Supper'll be in a couple of hours, but you can practice till then."

"Yes, ma'am. And thank you so much for the very best birthday I've ever had."

The next two hours seemed like minutes. But when Laura heard Miss Emma call her for supper, she put the lid down over the piano keys, jumped from the bench and hurried to the dining-room.

"Guess what, Miss Emma. I can do the scales without lookin', and I can put my fingers on the keys with my eyes closed. I even tried a couple of the songs in the book and was able to play by reading the notes." Laura plopped into her chair. "Thank you, thank you for lettin' me play, and for showin' me where my fingers go."

For supper, Miz Mary served thick steaks, baked potatoes covered with butter, carrots cooked in brown sugar and slabs of warm bread. After one bite of the tender meat,

Laura proclaimed steak her new favorite food. The meal was flavored with continuous conversation about music. Miss Emma shared more piano tips, as well as more basics for playing stringed instruments and the accordion, while Laura listened with rapt attention, seldom interrupting even to ask questions.

When Miss Emma finished eating, she stood up and stepped away from the table, "I'm glad you had a good day so far, Laura, but I have a couple of surprises for you. I'll be right back." She walked into the parlor and came back holding a box with a big red ribbon. "Happy Birthday," she said, handing Laura the box.

"What a pretty ribbon. Thank you," Laura caressed the silky fabric. At Emma's urging, she removed the ribbon and opened the box. Inside she found a shiny, brand new pair of boots.

"They're the same size as the ones I loaned you, so they should fit. Good boots make a big difference when you're working outside or riding," Emma said.

"Oh, they're beautiful." Laura stroked the smooth, dark leather, then traced the graceful design swirls on the sides with her fingers. "Ain't never had new boots before. Thank you, Miss Emma. I promise to take good care of them."

"I know you will." Miss Emma cleared her throat, then reached into her trouser pocket and pulled out an envelope. "But I've got one more thing for you. Martha sent me a letter with this inside, a letter for you from Ruth."

Laura gasped, then reached for the envelope. She recognized her sister's handwriting and started to cry. She unfolded the letter with trembling fingers, and read it through twice, first to herself, then again out loud to Miss Emma.

Dear Laura,

I miss you so much, but it helps knowing you're with Miss Emma. Miz Carpenter told me lots of stories about her, and about the farm where they grew up, and it sounds really nice.

You left just in time. Pa came here, yelling and cussing, about an hour after you left. If Mr. Carpenter hadn't been here with Paul and me, no telling what he might have done to me.

Mr. Carpenter told him that if he ever

tried to bother me again, he'd tell the sheriff what he did to you. Pa looked about ready to bust, but left after that.

I see Lizbeth and sometimes Becca at the store. They're doing alright, mainly because they help each other. Ben gets more like Pa every time I see him.

I've only seen Bonnie once, when both girls came to town and brought her with them. She's too scared to walk to school by herself, so Lizbeth and Becca are planning to teach her at home.

Paul and I are getting married on October 1st. Sure wish you could be here. Won't be anybody from our family because I don't want Pa there and he won't let the girls come. I've got to get this done, so will say goodbye. Paul says goodbye too and that he's proud of you.

Love always, Your sister,

Ruth Cavanaugh (soon Ruth Carpenter!)

Laura folded the letter after reading it out loud, ignoring the tears than streaked her face, and the way her whole body was shaking. Then she ran to Miss Emma and threw her arms around her in a tight embrace. She held on with all her might. Miss Emma hugged right back and kissed the top of her head.

"Thank you, Miss Emma. This is the best birthday I've ever had."

CHAPTER SEVENTEEN

Self-Defense & Nightmares

October 1916, Two months later

"Good morning, Miss Laura," Miz Mary said, when Laura sat down at the table, surprised not to see Miss Emma in her usual place.

"Good morning to you too, Miz Mary. That smells so good." Laura inhaled the fragrant steam from a stack of johnnycakes smothered in butter and syrup. "Miss Emma already gone?"

"Yes, ma'am. She asked me to tell you that Eli needs you to ride today, helpin' herd cows, so you should go straight to the barn after breakfast."

It didn't take Laura long to finish eating,

then go back upstairs to change. About ten minutes later she headed to the barn, wearing boots, trousers, a long-sleeved shirt, a handkerchief tied around her neck, and a wide-brimmed hat. She had her hair in tight braids to keep it out of the way and also had her sheathed knife tucked into her right boot. Miss Emma had taught her to always have a knife ready on the farm since you never knew when you might need it.

Laura loved spending the day riding. Pa never thought girls could ever be good on a horse. He'd be surprised to see her now. She smiled, then remembered what Pa would think about her in trousers. Trousers sure beat tryin' to ride in a skirt.

When Laura entered the barn, Eli was standing near the barn door, hands on his hips. He reminded her of Miz Mary, with his dark hair, short, stocky body, and wizened round face. Did people who were married forever end up looking alike? Eli and Miz Mary sure did. Laura couldn't imagine what Miss Emma would do without Miz Mary taking care of the kitchen and Eli as the foreman of the farm.

"Hurry up, Miss Laura," Eli said, when

she entered the barn. "Ever'body else is already mounted up in the corral. I had Sam saddle up George for you, I know he's your favorite."

"Thanks." Eli and Laura marched through the barn, then out into the corral at the back. Sam, Eli's second in command, was holding George's reins. Several other riders were ready to go.

Laura mounted George, a big, feisty, paint gelding that she rode whenever she had the chance. "Aren't you comin' with us, Eli?" Laura asked when she noticed Eli remained on foot.

"Can't this time, Miss Laura, but Sam'll take good care of things." Eli looked at Sam, who nodded and tipped his hat in response. "Don't like to have you ridin' with the men, but today there's no other way to get the cattle moved. Stay close to Sam, and if you have any trouble, let him know right away."

"I will," Laura said, a little nervous at the prospect of depending on Sam. It would feel strange to ride without Eli. She'd never done it before, but she was a good rider and could handle herself. Besides, Eli wouldn't let her go if he didn't think he could trust Sam.

Laura looked at Sam, wishing she felt

confident with him as her protector. She knew he was Eli's right-hand man, but they couldn't have been more different. How could Laura ask him for something when he hardly ever talked? Sam was built like a beanpole, tall and skinny. And pale? He looked like he never got out in the sun even though Laura knew he did.

Sam nodded to Eli, then wheeled his horse around and trotted across the corral to where five other riders waited. Laura recognized three of them, but two were strangers. They only a few years older than Laura, both with scraggly brown hair and wispy beards, enough alike to be brothers. They sat a little way from the others, whispering as they watched Sam and Laura approach.

"Alright, you'all. We have to move the herd to the northeast pasture since they've purt near cleaned out the one where they are now. They're not goin' to want to go, so you'll have to watch 'em real careful like, or they'll sneak around and double back. No big rush, and no rough stuff, but we need to get the job done today."

Instructions given, Sam turned his horse and kneed him into a fast trot out of the corral gate. Laura was the fifth rider in line, with the two strangers trailing behind her. She could feel them staring at her, a creepy crawling sensation. Somethin' about them gave her the willies.

Laura could hear the two men's horses moving close together, right behind her. She sped up a little, but they kept pace with her. George seemed to sense her anxiety, shaking his head and twisting his ears forward and back.

"Look at that girl. Um, Um, never seen no girl on horseback workin' cows right along with men before." The voice had a whisper-like husky quality, just loud enough for Laura to hear.

"Me, neither. But then, with those braids, and ridin' that big old paint, she kind'a looks like a injun to me." The second man behind her snickered, then continued. "And ever'body knows those squaws can ride."

Laura could hear their words but knew that none of the riders in front could. She missed Eli's presence and wished Sam wasn't so far away.

Injun? Squaw? Laura didn't know why they were saying that, but she sure didn't like the way those two sounded. She squeezed George's sides, urging him to speed up and get closer to Sam and the others.

"Look, Daniel, she's tryin' to get away from us." Laughter followed the words, but it didn't sound funny to Laura.

"You're right, Frank, and that's not very friendly," the voice Laura now knew was Daniel said.

Frank chuckled. "Oh, I'll bet if she got to know us she'd be a lot more friendly. 'Course, I wouldn't care if she was friendly or not, iffen we could just get hold of her."

"Got that right. Love to have those legs wrapped around me like she's got 'em 'round that horse." Daniel said, a growly sound in his voice. He no longer laughed.

Laura had heard enough. Her heart raced. The reins were slick in her sweaty hands. She kicked George hard, keeping him at a gallop until she passed the other riders, slowing down only when she was next to Sam. He didn't ask any questions, so she didn't say a word, but stayed by his side until they reached the herd.

The riders spread themselves behind the cows, spaced out so they could bunch the animals closer together and move them in the right direction. Once the herd was in motion toward the new pasture, the riders paced behind making sure none of the animals strayed too far off to the sides. The work was slow, dirty, and took several hours to move the plodding creatures to their new pasture.

When the tired riders headed back to the barn, Laura found Daniel and Frank on either side of her with Sam nowhere in sight. She sped up to get away from them, but they matched her speed and moved in closer. She rose up in the stirrups, trying to see where Sam and the others were, but they were out of sight. George flipped his ears back and tossed his mane, feeling her agitation through the reins.

"You do look fine on that horse," Daniel's voice came from behind, on Laura's right side. "But then, I'll bet you look fine all the time."

Laura didn't respond, hoping they'd leave her alone.

"Come on, don't be like that." This time Frank was talking to her, about the same distance behind, but from her left. "We're just tryin' to be sociable."

Laura ignored the words as she once again urged George to speed up. She was breathing in shallow pants, and her heart raced faster in time with his hooves.

The maneuver didn't work. In minutes Daniel and Frank were even with her, one on each side. The three horses continued to gallop at full speed, wet patches forming on their sides and froth starting to form at the sides of their mouths.

Then Daniel and Frank's mounts moved closer on each side, trapping Laura between them. Frank leaned in from her left and grabbed George's bridle, forcing his head to the side and slowing him to a stop. At the same time Daniel reached out and placed his hand on Laura's right knee.

Both men were breathing hard and laughing as their horses pressed tight against George. "Might as well quit trying to run. We'll just catch you again," Daniel said, moving his hand up Laura's knee to the top of her thigh.

"That's right, sugar, nobody's in sight and we got you now." Frank giggled, then reached out and touched Laura's breast.

Laura didn't hear a single word either

man said, only a rushing sound in her ears. Her skin crawled, and her mind flashed back to Pa's face above her, then to Ben's whispered threats as he pulled her nightgown away. She pushed Daniel's hand off her leg, reached down and pulled the knife from her boot, and slashed the blade across the back of his hand.

"Aaaggh! Dammit it, you bitch, you cut me." Daniel yelled, lifting his bleeding hand against his chest.

When Daniel screamed, Frank tried to reach across her and grab the knife, but Laura whirled around and stabbed Frank's forearm. He screamed and jerked his arm back, giving Laura the chance to get away. George, spooked by the screaming and the smell of blood, bolted at full speed.

Laura couldn't believe she'd done that. She'd cut them, but she didn't know how bad. Both of 'em were bleeding. And Laura wasn't sorry. She hoped Miss Emma wouldn't send her away, but no way was any man going to grab her again.

Laura never slowed George down until she reached the safety of the barn. They were both sweating and breathing hard, caked in dust from the ride. "Sorry to push you so hard, but thanks for getting me out of there." Laura petted George's face and sides after removing the saddle and bridle.

She was still leaning into his warm body, both taking comfort from the contact, when she heard hoofbeats entering the barn. Laura hoped the three hired hands she knew were approaching, but it was Sam, followed by Daniel and Frank.

"Darn fools, you know better'n getting messed up in barbed wire. I'll never know how you both got cut, though. Your story don't make no sense," Sam said. "Clean yourselves up then take care of the horses."

Laura kept her face against George, listening to the men dismount. "Miss Laura," Sam said when he spotted her standing next to George. "Come on, I'll walk you to the house. These morons'll take care of George."

Without a glance at Daniel or Frank, Laura walked out of the barn with Sam at her side. She kept her face impassive but was shaking so hard she was sure Sam could see. He never said a word, though, even when he tipped his hat and left her at the porch.

Sam had to know something happened out there. Laura hoped he wouldn't tell Eli, 'cause she didn't want to talk about it. "I'm not sorry though," she said to herself. "I'm not sorry at all."

It took Laura awhile to get cleaned up, but a plate of food waited for her on the table. With the huge lump of fear in her throat, she choked most of the food down. When she carried her plate and utensils out to the kitchen, she found Eli and Miz Mary waiting for her.

Miz Mary's mouth was clenched in a tight, straight line, but it was Eli who spoke. "Miss Laura, I know those two men didn't get hurt on no barbed wire. You cut 'em, didn't you?"

Laura leaned against the table for support. "I didn't mean to hurt 'em, but they were sayin' awful things and grabbin' me."

"That's what I was afraid of. You're not in trouble, but if I could I'd shoot 'em for what they did. I'm lettin' them go, but with the threat of gettin' horsewhipped if they ever show their faces around here again. It's my fault for sendin' you out. No excuse. You'll not ride herd again unless I'm with you."

Sudden tears pooled in Laura's eyes. "Thank you.

What'd Miss Emma say?"

"Miss Emma won't say a thing when I tell her Ihad to fire those two. She trusts my judgment with the hired hands. Unless you want to talk to her about this, I don't see no reason to bring it up."

Laura sighed, sagging back against the table. Miz Mary gathered Laura into her arms for a hug, then she and Eli left the kitchen and headed to their quarters.

She was glad they didn't have to tell Miss Emma. Laura knew Miss Emma would say that words don't hurt nobody, and that if you didn't trust somebody, you should stay away from 'em. Laura didn't think Miss Emma'd be mad about her using the knife, 'cause she also always said, "You got to learn to protect yourself." Laura just wished she hadn't gotten so scared.

Laura went up to her room and fell asleep almost as soon as her head touched the pillow. But morning found her completely exhausted, her body twisted in the quilt as though she'd been running and fighting all night.

She couldn't believe that her nightmares were back after so many months of peaceful sleep. Pa and Ben kept poppin' out of the bushes and chasing her, always gettin' closer and closer. Then Pa would be on top of her again, but his face would change into Ben, then it'd be Daniel and Frank. She was terrified, but nobody could hear her screaming. Why had the nightmares returned? And why were they worse than before?. She wished she could ask somebody about them, but Miss Emma said not to talk about personal things like that to anybody. Laura didn't believe she could bear having to live with those nightmares again and hoped with all her heart that they'd go away.

Laura never saw Daniel or Frank again, but they joined Pa and Ben to torment her almost every night in her sleep for the next few months. She tried working herself to the point of exhaustion, but that didn't seem to make a difference.

The one thing that helped was spending time in the music room, losing herself in the melodies. Laura played the piano whenever she had free time in the evening after she finished her chores. She was sitting on the bench practicing chords one day when Miss Emma brought Laura a second letter from Ruth.

Dear Laura,

Can you believe I'm a married woman now? Paul and I are very, very happy. Wish you and our sisters could have been at the wedding, but I hope you know we were thinking about you.

We're living upstairs above the store, in the apartment with Paul's parents. It's a little crowded, but we all get along. One day Paul and I hope to build a house of our own.

Wish I could give you news about Lizbeth and Becca, but it seems Ben is always with them now when they come to town. They can't talk to me, but at least I can see them. Haven't seen Bonnie, though, but I'm sure they are taking good care of her.

Not too much new to tell you about folks in town, except there's lots of talk about the country maybe going to war. Now that England is involved, lots of folks think President Wilson won't be able to keep us out. It scares me to think of Paul joining up, but nothing I can do but wait.

Remember Mr. Gentry, the manager of

the Bank? Well, he bought one of the new horseless carriages. It was the first in town, but within two weeks three more families bought them, too. Don't know the people very well because they're new in town, but they must have plenty of money. I think they work for the railroad.

Oh, yes, there is one exciting thing. Our town will soon have its own post office, and it will be located inside our store! Mr. Carpenter did all the paperwork to apply months ago, and it was finally approved. That will make it much easier to send letters to you since I'll have the post office right here.

Good bye for now, take care of yourself. Love always,

Your sister, Ruth Carpenter

CHAPTER EIGHTEEN

How Much More

April 1918, Eighteen Months later

T he letters came much more often after the new post office opened for business in the store, one about every other month. Laura loved hearing from Ruth, and reread each letter over and over until the next arrived. They were always short, but she treasured the snippets of information about the family.

Ruth's letter in June was a complete surprise, telling Laura that Lizbeth had gotten married. Not to a young man who courted her, but to a man their father's age whose wife had died and left him with four small children. It sounded like Lizbeth had accepted the arrangement as a way to escape from their Pa. While Laura was happy for her to get out, she worried even more about Becca and Bonnie.

Becca had always been so close to Lizbeth, how could she cope as the oldest girl with all the responsibilities of running the household? How on earth could Becca manage without Lizbeth? She must have felt betrayed and abandoned when Lizbeth left since the two had always done everything together. And Bonnie? Left alone with weak Becca and Ben? Becca couldn't protect herself, much less their baby sister. Laura was once again overwhelmed with guilt for escaping alone, leaving Bonnie behind.

When the next letter arrived, Laura was eager for more details, but was shocked to learn that Pa had a new wife.

Pa married Sarah Winters? She was in the same grade in school as Becca. Why would Sarah agree to marry Pa? Bet he asked her pa first, and she was pressured into it. Laura remembered Sarah. She was a mousy, quiet little girl, hardly ever said a thing. Laura guessed she'd be a help to Becca, but how could she protect Bonnie?

In between letters, Laura continued learning from Miss Emma, who quizzed her on stories in the weekly newspapers, and taught her music each day after they finished all their work. Laura was equally at home with outside chores and working in the house, but she never could seem to master cooking, in spite of Miz Mary's best efforts.

Then in February, a letter arrived that caused Laura to shout with excitement.

Dear Laura,

Christmas was wonderful, but Paul and I missed you.

I saw Lizbeth at the store this morning and got to talk to her some. Ben was in town and saw us through the door, but all he could do was make a mean face. At least she's safe from Pa and Ben, even if her life is hard. She said Mr. Perkins is alright, not mean like Pa. She really cares about the children but looks awful frazzled.

Haven't seen Becca for quite awhile because Pa sends Sarah in for his supplies now. I guess Becca has to stay with Bonnie. Poor Sarah, she's too scared to say anything, and her eyes skitter around like she's afraid to look at anybody. I've seen bruises on her face and arms, so Pa hasn't changed.

Now for the best news. Miz Martha and I are coming to visit in April, and we'll stay a few days. Miz Martha misses Miss Emma something fierce, and I can't wait to see you. And I'll be able to answer those million questions you've got for me.

Good bye for now, take care of yourself.
Love always,
Your sister, Ruth Carpenter

Laura glanced at Miss Emma across the table strewn with papers, face beaming. "They're comin', they're comin' in April."

"Who's comin'? Slow down and tell me."

"Miz Martha and Ruth are coming to visit in April." Miss Emma was as thrilled as Laura. They spent the next weeks cleaning and polishing everything in the house and chasing the tiniest spiderwebs hidden in corners of the high ceilings. Miz Mary baked all of Miz Martha's favorites. Even though the house always looked clean and organized, Miss Emma wanted everything flawless for her sister. The hired hands helped too, making sure every field was neat as can be, every building was freshly whitewashed, and all the animals looked their best.

"Miss Emma," Laura shouted as she scampered down the stairs, "they're coming. I saw 'em through the window."

"They'll still be a good while if you looked out the bedroom window," Miss Emma said, chuckling at Laura's enthusiasm. "Go on out to the porch and watch. I'll let Miz Mary and Eli know it won't be long now."

Laura didn't need any more encouragement. She raced out the door and settled on the porch railing. She couldn't believe she would get to see Ruth again after more than two years.

Soon Miss Emma joined Laura, both focused on the wagon they could see in the distance. Unable to stay still, they ran down into the yard before the wagon stopped.

"Ruth, Ruth," Laura called and waved, then rushed to her sister's side, reaching up to help her down. "I can't believe you're really here."

The minute Ruth stepped down from the wagon, she and Laura were in each other's arms. Their attention was focused on one another, or they would've seen Miz Martha and Miss Emma hugging on the other side of the wagon, just as excited about their reunion.

"Come on inside," Miss Emma said. "Eli will be right out to tend to the horse and take your bags upstairs. Miz Mary fixed a special dinner for us, so let's go on in."

Laura kept hold of Ruth's hand until they reached the table, then perched on the edge of the chair next to her.

"You look so pretty, Ruth, but you feel a lot thicker in the middle than I remember. Being married is making you fat."

Ruth burst out laughing. "I'm not getting fat, I'm gonna have a baby."

"A baby." Miss Emma and Laura shouted at the same time and leapt from their chairs. Ruth and Miz Martha jumped up, too, then all four were hugging one another. When Miz Mary brought the first platters of food in and heard the news, she jumped up and down and clapped her hands, celebrating right along with the others.

Once things quieted down, and they began to eat, Laura turned to Ruth and said, "How does Paul feel about the baby? Will it be alright with him if it's a girl?"

"Paul's as happy as can be, and he doesn't

care what we have. In fact, he's been saying he'd like to have a little girl that looks just like me. I know what you're thinking, but Paul's not like Pa."

Thank goodness Paul was different. Ruth was so lucky. "Do the girls know?"

"No, we haven't told anybody in town, yet. 'Sides, don't hardly see any of 'em except Lizbeth anymore." Ruth's smile disappeared. "So many changes since you left."

"It's hard to imagine Lizbeth as a married woman, and to such an old man," Laura said. "And her as a ma to four young'uns. She always worked together with Becca. I don't see how she can handle everything all by herself."

"I know. Lizbeth says she's happy, leastways, she's happier than she was being with Pa, especially after you got away. She said he was crazy mad for a long time, and took it out on everybody," Ruth shook her head, and sighed. "Mr. Perkins loved his first wife, and bout near fell apart when she died. He seems grateful to have Lizbeth for the little ones. She says he's been very kind and patient with her."

"That left Becca running the house." Laura said. "Don't see how she's managed."

"No, Becca couldn't manage alone. Guess

Pa knew that too, 'cause he married Sarah right after Lizbeth left. Poor thing. Heard tell Pa talked to her pa first, and she didn't have enough gumption to say no."

"That's kind a what I figured when I read the news in your letter. I remember Sarah Winters from school. She's younger than Lizbeth, just about Becca's age." Laura was still horrified by the thought of such a young girl married to her pa.

"I know, and I feel the same way. But she knows how to run a house, being the oldest in her family, and that's what Pa wanted." Ruth picked at the food on her plate. "Sure feel sorry for her, though. When she comes in the store, she hardly looks at anybody. When she talks she always raises her hands to her face like she's trying to hide. Poor little thing looks like a scared rabbit."

No one spoke for awhile, each focused on their own thoughts as they finished the meal. After Miz Mary cleared the table, the four strolled out onto the porch and settled onto old, cushioned rocking chairs.

"Ruth, what about Bonnie? How's she doing with all the changes?" Laura asked.

"Let's go take a walk. I'm kind a tired

sitting so long." Ruth stood up, and exchanged a long, silent look with Miz Martha. "You and Miss Emma can catch up while Laura shows me around the garden and barn."

Laura followed Ruth down the porch steps, a little surprised that they were leaving the others, but happy to be with her sister.

Ruth didn't say a word until they reached the fenced corral behind the barn. She rested her arms on the top fence rail, watching some mares and their foals in the pasture. After a few minutes, she sighed, turned to Laura and said, "There's no easy way to say this, so I'll just spit it out. Honey, Bonnie died."

"No," Laura begged. "Please, no, don't say that. She can't be dead."

Ruth didn't say a word, but the look of pity on her face shattered Laura's hope.

"No. Oh God, please no. It's my fault. I never should have left her."

"It's not your fault. It was just a freak accident." "Yes, it is my fault. I always watched out for her. If

I'd been there, she'd still be alive." Laura sobbed deep gulping cries, as she backed away, then turned and stumbled to the barn.

I'm so sorry, Bonnie. So sorry. I saved

myself but left you alone. That was wrong and selfish. I should've taken you with me. I should have found a way.

Laura circled around inside the barn until she found a dark, hidden corner behind a tall stack of bags stuffed full of grain and dropped to her knees. She closed her eyes, but somehow found herself in another place, in Pa's barn, watching a horrific scene unfold.

In her mind she knew she was hidden in a corner of Miss Emma's barn, but it was like being in two places at once. Her eyes were shut, but it was as if she was an invisible witness to the events she saw unfold.

Ruth found her kneeling, bent over, arms clasped around her torso. Laura was no longer crying, but moaning in pain, making a guttural, heart wrenching sound Ruth had never heard before.

"Ben did it. Oh God, Ben killed Bonnie," Laura whispered.

"No, don't say that. It was an accident. Why would you say such a horrible thing?" Ruth asked.

"Because I just saw what took place. I closed my eyes and watched everything happen, plain as day," Laura didn't look up.

She remained in the same curled position as if in agony. "I saw Sarah and Becca hoeing weeds in the garden, talking and laughing as they worked down the rows. Bonnie had finished muckin'out the barn and was spreading clean straw in the stalls.

Everyone thought Ben was away mending fences, but he'd come back 'cause he needed another roll of wire. He saw Bonnie go into the barn, and knew the others couldn't see him. It wasn't the first time he'd caught Bonnie alone and forced himself on her. She never told anybody, because he scared her into keeping quiet. He sneaked up on her in the barn and shoved her down into the straw. Bonnie couldn't push him off her, so she tried to scream for help. Ben put his hand over her mouth to keep her quiet. Then he raped her, pounding her poor little body hard into the straw, keepin' his hand over her face the whole time. He didn't even notice that his hand covered her nose too. When she struggled to breathe, he just thought she was trying to get away, and kept holding her down." Laura stopped to take a deep breath, then continued.

Ruth shook her head back and forth in denial, hands pressed against her mouth. She backed away from Laura as if trying to escape the awful words.

"Ben didn't kill her on purpose, but he did kill her. When he saw what he'd done, he fixed her clothes back in place, carried her up the ladder to the hayloft, then threw her body down. He knew no one would find her for awhile, so he could ride away and act surprised when he got back. He was scared that somebody might figure out what'd happened to her before she fell. So, two days later he told Pa he wanted to join the Army to fight the Germans, and left."

Ruth dropped her hands from her face, wrapping her arms around herself. Her face was ashen, all the color having drained away. "How did you know? I never told you Bonnie fell from the hayloft and was found dead. Fact is, I didn't tell you anything about how she died. How did you know Ben wasn't there when it happened? And how on earth did you know Ben left to join the Army two days later?"

"Don't know. I just saw it like it was happening right in front of me, and inside I know it's true."

"I don't know whether or not it's all true,

but you're right about a lot, and there ain't no normal way for you to know."

Ruth stared at her sister, then said. "Laura, you can't tell anyone what you just told me. Folks would think you're crazy. Some church folks might even say you're possessed or something. Promise me you won't tell a soul. Even if you're right, telling this story won't help Bonnie, but could hurt you bad. Promise me, swear right now you won't ever repeat that story."

Laura nodded as fresh tears ran down her face and dripped from her chin.

"I'm so sorry, Laura. I don't want to hurt you even more, but we've got to keep this between us. We gotta go back in a minute, but Miz Martha and Miss Emma will figure we both look sad cause I told you about Bonnie. You can't say nothing more than that."

Laura just nodded, too heartbroken to even speak. Ruth knelt down on the ground, wrapped her arms around Laura's shoulders, and rocked her back and forth.

After a long time, they stood up and walked back to the house together, arms entwined around one another's waists.

The rest of the afternoon dragged by. Laura felt disconnected as if everyone was moving in slow motion. Sounds around her— dogs barking, birdcalls, voices of the hands floating in the wind—were muted, and everything looked strange, as if washed out and devoid of color. She tried hard to stay focused since relaxing meant slipping back into the horrific vision she'd glimpsed earlier.

The two sets of sisters talked, even smiled sometimes, but Laura's mood was blanketed by the sorrow and pain of Bonnie's death. After a light supper, they moved outside again to the rockers on the porch.

"It hardly seems possible that Laura's been here for two years," Miz Martha glanced at her sister. "Thank you so much for taking her in."

"Don't need to thank me. It was the right thing to do," Miss Emma said. "Laura's good company and a good worker. I'm gonna miss her when she turns eighteen and moves on."

"Moves on?" Ruth sounded shocked.

"Of course," Miss Emma said. "I'm happy to help a young'un in need, but when she's a grown woman, it'll be time for her to find her own way. Not much chance of meeting a beau out here or in the tiny towns nearby, so probably best for her to go to Tulsa where there's lots of growing companies that are always hiring workers. She'll need a safe place to live, too, and Tulsa has plenty of hotels where young, single women can be safe living alone."

Moving away? Two years from now? Moving to a city? Laura heard all that was said around her, but didn't feel like a part of the conversation, even though it was about her. She had questions, but not enough energy to ask them out loud.

"Excuse me, but I'm going on up to my room now. I'm awful tired, and kind of need some time alone," Laura said.

"But Laura, I thought you'd like to play the piano for Miz Ruth and Miz Martha," Emma said, surprised to see Laura stand up and take a step toward the door.

"I'm sorry, but I don't feel much like music tonight, Miss Emma. I'll play for everyone tomorrow."

Laura trudged through the living room and up the stairs, but stopped in the doorway to her room.

Bonnie would have loved a room like this, all clean and bright. Now she'll never, ever have a place of her own. Never know what it feels like to sleep in a real bed, with a feather pillow and a quilt with bright colors that haven't been washed out. She'll never have a window with pretty yellow curtains, or a washbasin and a pitcher with bright flowers painted on the glass. It just wasn't fair. She was the littlest, the baby of the family, and never should've died like that.

With those thoughts, the dam inside Laura's chest broke, and her pain poured out through tears that scalded her skin. It was too hard to remain standing, so she moved to the white rocker and sat down. She leaned her head back and closed her eyes, then cried until she was cried out. She never made a sound, exhausted clear through to her soul.

Startled, Laura woke up stiff and sore from sleeping in the chair, and in a room that was dark and quiet. She had no idea how much time had passed, but through the window the only light she saw was the moon high overhead. She changed into a nightgown, washed her face, and climbed into bed.

Laura's mind spun in circles as she lay there, unable to fall back to sleep.

Bonnie was dead because Laura had run away and left her. Ben raped and killed her little sister. How could he do that? She had to leave in two years and start all over in a big city. How could she do that? If she had to find a job and a place to live, what could she tell people about her life? Miss Emma told her never to let anyone know she was half Indian. Shouldn't even say where she'd come from, since she ran away. And never, ever let anyone know she'd been raped, because they'd think she was loose. Ruth told her never to talk about what happened to Bonnie in the barn, or folks might think she was possessed by the devil.

Laura raised up and twisted to the side, placing her feet on the floor. It was hard to move, and her whole body was cold with pain and fear.

Was there somethin' wrong with her? Did she cause all the things that happened? She didn't think so. She couldn't figure out what she might have done to cause Pa, or Ben to do what they did. But what if she was wrong? Even Frank and Daniel must have seen something bad in her. Everybody says no normal man would attack his own kin unless she did something to cause it. And two total strangers? Was it her fault for what they did?

"You did nothing wrong, Laura." The voice was clear and strong and sounded somewhat familiar.

Laura looked around, but there was no one in the room. She was hearing the words inside her head, sort of like when she saw the vision earlier. But not really in her head at all, more like the sound was part of the air in the room, pulsing all around and through her at the same time. She felt the words as much as she heard them.

"Bonnie's safe now with me, and Ben will have to live with what he did to her every day for the rest of his life."

Laura rose up off the bed and turned in circles around the room, trying to comprehend the source of the words that engulfed her.

"Ma? Ma? Is that you? How is this happening?

I must be crazy, thinking I'm hearing your voice."

"You're not crazy, but you are special.

I'm always with you, and I'll always watch over you. Rest easy now. Your courage brought you this far, and your strength will carry you through the days and years ahead."

Laura sighed, went back to the bed and rested, sitting on the edge. She no longer cared where the voice was coming from or if it really was Ma. All that mattered was the comforting sense of warmth and tranquility that surrounded her.

Acknowledgments

Books are not created in a vacuum, and I owe huge debts of gratitude to a wide variety of supporters for helping bring this one to completion.

My husband, Stan, and daughter Sheryl are always my greatest fans, somehow remaining patient and understanding when I ignore them while trying to get a difficult section worked out. Without them, it would be impossible. I love them both more than I can express.

My parents, Al and June Azevedo, are always willing to read and reread rough drafts, giving praise whether it's deserved or not. I'll always try to be worthy of their pride and love.

I owe huge thanks to a delightful and talented mother and daughter team, Sue Clark, and her daughter Leslie Clark. Thank you, Sue, for your patience and guidance in editing, and Leslie for your patience and understanding as you created the cover. I am blessed with the friendship and assistance of a wonderful community of writers in the Sacramento area. The members of the Northern California Publishers & Authors have taught me more than I imagined possible when I first joined the group. Gini Grossenbacher, a wonderful writer, teacher, and leader of an amazing critique group, not only helped teach me the difference between writing fiction and non-fiction but has become a dear friend.

The last group I must thank are those marvelous, patient readers who went through my drafts and shared their comments and suggestions. Some are writers, some are avid readers, but all of them mean the world to me. Here are a few of their names: Betty Smith, Norma Jean Thornton, Carla Bowman, Karen Simon, Michelle Hamilton, Lila Devi, Vivienne Brocklehurst, and Teresa Klimek. I know I'm forgetting some names, but please forgive me—my memory may be faulty sometimes, but I appreciate each and every one of you more than you know.

About the Author

I've been passionate about three things my whole life, reading, flying, and animals.

I was one of those kids who walked down the halls holding an open book, glancing up to keep from running into people or walls. I no longer read walking down the street, but I do manage to read a few sentences on my Kindle at red lights. Reading is as important to me as breathing, and one of my greatest joys now as an author is getting to know other writers. What could be more awesome than reading a fantastic book and being friends with the writer?

Thanks to a fantastic husband who knows how much I love flying, I've been up in a hot air balloon, a two-man helicopter, a glider, and an open cockpit bi-plane. He even encouraged me to get my private pilot's license, but I had to quit when the economy crashed in 2008. Every minute in the air was amazing, and today I'd go up in anything, with anyone willing to take me, anytime, and anywhere. No wonder one of my writing idols is Richard Bach, pilot and author of *Jonathan Livingston Seagull* and my favorite book ever, *Illusions, The Adventures of a Reluctant Messiah*. My love of animals made me want to be a veterinarian, but I fell in love and married during my first year of college. In spite of dropping out, I've still managed to make a contribution to animals by raising 514 bottle-fed kittens, working an all-volunteer cat spay and neuter clinic every month for over 20 years, and writing books about animal rescue.

I believe that a supportive family is key to a happy life and have been blessed with an understanding husband who has been my best friend and life partner for 54 years so far.

Sacramento, California has been home for most of my life. Stan and I live next door to my parents, and share our home with our cats Gracie, Portia, Ash, Bonnie, and Becca.

My philosophy of life is simple—if you can find harmony within, you can make a difference to the people around you. Life just gets better each year as long as you keep dreaming and loving.

I now have a favorite thing in life, writing! And one of the best parts of being a writer is hearing from readers. You can contact me through my website, https://www.sharonsdarrow.com, contact page,
my facebook page https://www.facebook.com/SamatiPress/,
my LinkedIn page https://www.linkedin.com/in/sharondarrow/,
or my personal email address, sharon@sharonsdarrow.com.
If you have something to share about strong women in your life, or comments about my books, I'd love to hear from you.

And don't forget that reviews are incredibly important to writers. If you enjoyed this book, please leave your review on Amazon, Goodreads, or any other place you can. If you didn't like it, please keep your opinion to yourself—just kidding, if you didn't like it, I'd love to hear from you personally so I can understand and do a better job writing in the future.

If you'd like to know what happens to Laura and her family next, turn the page for a preview of the second book in the Laura's Dash Series, *Strive and Protect*, which is available through my website and all the usual online outlets.

CHAPTER ONE
Betrayal

November 1923

Laura was excited throughout dinner, eager to see the highest rated movie of the year. She skipped rather than strolled at Bruce's side when they finished eating and headed toward the Argosy. Bruce had parked the car, a shiny black Buick Touring Car convertible, and his most prized possession, a block away from the cafe.

The theater's large marque announced The Covered Wagon, in huge letters. The names J. Warren Kerrigan and Lois Wilson, stars of the film, appeared right below the title in smaller letters. Bruce gave their tickets to the usher at the door, then led Laura into the opulent interior.

Laura's low-heeled shoes sank into thick maroon carpeting. Heavy tapestries hung on the walls between glass cases containing posters for upcoming feature films, and muffled the whispered conversations around her. Soon they settled in plush seats, waiting for the heavy curtains to rise.

She was glad the interior was dim after being surrounded by pretty women that made her feel almost dowdy by comparison. They wore shimmering silk and satin, accented by fur wraps and feather bedecked hats. Her favorite forest green wool frock with pale gold at the cuffs, collar, and narrow band accenting the dropped waist above narrow pleats seemed ordinary and plain. Her patterned black stockings and cloche hat sporting a pale gold bow couldn't compare to sleek, silken hosiery and high fashion hats.

Laura took a shallow breath—all she could manage with the tight brassiere that compressed her chest—and gazed at the heavy velvet curtains. She resolved to think only of the movie and the handsome man next to her.

Laura's attention never wavered from the film, entranced from the movie title to the closing credits. She loved movies and the magnificent music and sound effects produced by the magnificent Wurlitzer theater organ. Her fingers danced over imaginary keys along with the organist seated at the gold and black console in the orchestra pit.

"That was the bees knees. No wonder it's the most popular movie around." Laura and Bruce maneuvered through the dense crowd. "Thank you so much for bringing me. Tonight has been the best evening ever."

"You're welcome." Bruce placed his arm around Laura's slim waist, holding her close even though she stiffened at his touch. At last, they got out of the theater and headed for the car.

"Let's find a quiet place to talk. I've got something important to ask you."

Laura's mood changed from excitement to worry in an instant. She cared about Bruce very much—in fact, sometimes she thought she might be in love with him—but his tone sounded serious. She stayed quiet until they got back into the car, listening for any clues to what was on his mind.

Bruce chattered about the movie, paying no attention to Laura's distracted responses. He parked the car near St. Thomas Catholic Church, then led Laura to a secluded bench under the trees on the park-like grounds.

"It's so peaceful here," Laura said, settling on a bench. She shivered a little, wondering what was coming.

"Yes, and perfect for us," Bruce said. "Hey, don't look so serious. I've got an exciting idea."

Laura tried to control her rapid breathing, waiting to hear what he had to say.

"What are you doing for Thanksgiving?" Bruce said.

"Uh, just having dinner in the dining hall, I guess," she said, a little surprised by the question. "Nothing special. The YWCA has a lot of rules, but we're not required to eat there. I could skip the Thanksgiving dinner if you want me to."

"Well, my family celebration should be over by three."

The family celebration? Is he inviting me to join them?

Bruce continued talking. "What would you say about us going to Oklahoma City for the weekend? If we left at three thirty, we could get there Thursday night, and then come back Sunday evening. I'll get us a room in the best hotel in town. We can do whatever you want for two whole, wonderful days." Bruce pulled her to him.

Laura shoved him away, not sure she understood what he'd said. "What? Are you asking me to join you for Thanksgiving dinner and then take a trip?"

"Wish I could, but my parents are old-fashioned. I've told them how much I care about you, but Mother is hung up on her society rules. She'd never be able to see past you being half Indian."

"How can you say you care about me? It sounds like your mother isn't the only one hung up on stupid society rules."

Bruce reached for her hand but Laura stayed out of range. "It's not just that. My father's most important goal is having me take over the bank when he's ready to retire, but he insists that I have to find a wife with the perfect pedigree or he won't pass it on to me."

Laura stood and stepped away from the bench, shaking her head in shocked disbelief.

"Don't be like that, doll. I'm in no hurry to settle down with some boring society debutante. I'd rather keep seeing you, and a weekend together would be so great, just the two of us." Bruce leaned forward and his voice thickened. "Say yes, baby, please. You know you want to."

Laura's emotions cycled from confusion and shame, to pain, then blinding anger. "You and your parents don't think I'm good enough to sit at your table, but you want to take me to a hotel in Oklahoma City? You can't even consider me for a wife, but I'd be okay as a girlfriend on the side?"

"Don't look like that," Bruce implored. "We've had fun together, and I just want to keep having fun. I never said anything about us being more than that."

Laura fought hard to keep from crying. "Going to a movie or having dinner is different from sharing a hotel room for the weekend. I can't imagine what I've done to make you think that would be okay."

She trembled from head to toe, throat burning. "Take me home, right now."

"Oh, come on. Stop acting like some kind of innocent little school girl. You told me your history. What's the problem? It's not like you're a virgin ... and with your own father yet."

Laura slapped Bruce as hard as she could, almost knocking him off the bench. "He raped me," she screamed. Her hand stung like fire, but the flaming red mark on Bruce's face was worth it.

Without saying a word, Laura ran away, back the way they'd come.

Bruce yelled. "Come back here, you little bitch. No girl hits me and gets away with it. Where the hell do you think you're going?"

"Leave me alone. I never want to see you again." Laura spit the words back over her shoulder.

"You know you don't mean that. Come here and I'll take you home." Bruce's words were softer, but his tone couldn't make up for what he'd said.

Laura ran even faster, staring straight ahead as she passed the ivy-covered stone walls of the church. She angled toward the road, sliding on the damp grass as she passed dark trees, lit only by the moonlight.

No more words pursued her, but Laura heard Bruce's car starting. When he drew even with her, Bruce leaned out the window and said, "It's a long way to the YWCA. Get in the car. You know I'm right."

Laura didn't turn her head or acknowledge him at all. Bruce drove alongside her and kept talking. Then he gave up and sped away. Only then did she slow down to a snail's pace, struggling to see through the tears that coursed down her face.

How could she have been so stupid? A handsome, rich guy like Bruce with his college education and a Father who owned a bank? Why, oh why had she trusted him?

Hot tears still fell as Laura reached the YWCA front door. She was late and had to listen to a lecture before being allowed to go to her room. Once there, Laura paced back and forth, from wall to wall, raging inside.

She pressed her hands into her temples, unable to keep the words inside. "What's the matter with you? Miss Emma warned you and warned you not to tell anyone about your past. They will use whatever you tell them to hurt and manipulate you."

Over and over the same phrases reverberated inside Laura's mind, even after she stopped speaking them aloud. At long last she stopped circling the room and sat down. She had only one choice, and that was to get as far away as possible. Tulsa was a big city with plenty of room to start over. She'd be smart this time. She'd gotten along just fine without a boyfriend before.

Decision made, Laura pulled her suitcase from under the bed and started to pack her things. She left fresh clothes for the morning on the dresser, together with her comb and toothbrush, set the clock for an hour before dawn, then climbed into bed.

www.ingramcontent.com/pod-product-compliance
Lightning Source LLC
Chambersburg PA
CBHW060621260626
47161CB00008B/2769